Lightning in the Blood

May 17

MARIE BRENNAN

LIGHTNING IN THE BLOOD

A TOM DOHERTY ASSOCIATES BOOK

NEW YORK

This is a work of fiction. All of the characters, organizations, and events portrayed in this novella are either products of the author's imagination or are used fictitiously.

LIGHTNING IN THE BLOOD

Cover art by Greg Ruth
Cover design by Christine Foltzer

Edited by Miriam Weinberg

A Tor.com Book
Published by Tom Doherty Associates
175 Fifth Avenue
New York, NY 10010

www.tor.com

Tor® is a registered trademark of
Macmillan Publishing Company, LLC.

ISBN 978-0-7653-9143-8 (ebook)
ISBN 978-0-7653-9201-5 (trade paperback)

First Edition: March 2017

Lightning in the Blood

The pass through which Ree came back into Solaike barely deserved the name. There was no road, though the valley below started off well enough, with level, easy terrain alongside a cool stream perfect for resting one's feet in—if her feet had needed rest. But the upper end mocked that flatness, the ground rising precipitously into a tangle of boulders and thick undergrowth. Only two things kept Ree going then: an instinctual belief that the deer track she was following *could* be traversed by some-one on two legs, and a perverse determination to do ex-actly that.

Determination won out over terrain. She hauled her-self to the top, panting and triumphant. And for her pains, she was rewarded with a splendid view across the Heliin mountains of Solaike, laid out under a brilliant, cloudless sky.

They weren't a large range, in either height or extent. But they were carpeted in a dense growth of trees, an emerald mask over a labyrinthine assortment of caves, outcroppings, and valleys you could only find by falling into them. Here and there a rock face broke through the mask, defying goats to attempt its heights. In this landscape, a band of rebels against the usurper Valtaja had held out for a generation, despite repeated attempts to dig them out. Looking at the place, it wasn't hard to see why.

Ree mostly knew the mountains from a lower vantage point, hiding out with those rebels, helping them with their war. She'd never seen the place from so high up. After a bit of searching, though, she found the notched peak of Ahvelu, and then she had a sense of where she was. Southwest of the main pass into Solaike—well, she'd known that much already, when she decided not to take the easy road—but not as far southwest as Veiss, where the rebels had overwhelmed the garrison three years ago and achieved the first major victory of their revolution.

If she'd had the sense the higher powers gave a chipmunk, she would have come via the main pass. But she'd spent the last few months in a city, and now she craved a bit of peace and quiet, away from people. And entering Solaike this way meant Aadet wouldn't know she was coming. She had a reputation for turning up when he least expected it; it would be a shame to break that streak now. She was masked, of course, but that didn't hide everything, and there were enough people who would remember and recognize her from the days of the revolution.

Besides, she liked the novelty of it. A path she'd never followed before, a view she'd never seen from quite this angle.

Now she had the challenge of figuring out how to get from here to Taraspai. By her reckoning, if she headed over a nearby ridge, she had good odds of striking one of the old quarry tracks that laced this area. During the days of the revolution, she never would have used any of those roads; a traveler on a known path made for an easy target. Something Valtaja's soldiers had learned all too well—but they feared the forest, hugging the roads and leaving them only with reluctance. There were leopards out there, and stories of worse things. If some of those worse things were just rebels in frightening disguises . . . did it make much of a difference? Dead was dead.

But the rebels were gone now, occupying the capital in triumph, and Ree didn't *always* have to take the hardest route. The novelty of descending slopes by falling down them ass-first wore off after a while. And by her estimate, she had at least two days' travel ahead of her before she got back to anything resembling civilization, even with a road to help—longer to reach the capital itself. She paused long enough to scrape her dark hair off her face and back into a fresh braid, then set out again.

Getting up and over that excuse for a pass had taken up half the day, and finding a path down the other side took most of the rest. Ree didn't have to sleep, but in these mountains, going on in the dark would have been asking for trouble. She was as capable of breaking her neck as any human. Or, for that matter, being eaten by some noctural predator. She spent a wary night perched high in a tree, sabre unsheathed in her hand, listening to the forest converse with itself in whispers and growls and brief, dying screams.

She came upon one of the tracks sooner than she expected the next morning. It ran in a general east-west direction, its rocky surface stitched together with thick weeds. Ree put her boots on it with a sense of relief and headed east. The road definitely made for easier going, but also hotter, with the sun beating down on her head. *Right. There's a reason why I don't usually come back to Solaike during the summer.*

She kept a sharp eye out as she walked. The revolution might be over, and the track showed no signs of recent traffic in any large numbers, but wariness was a habit carved into her bones. And even in this isolated region, she couldn't expect to be the only one around.

It wasn't even midday yet when Ree saw a telltale curl of smoke in the air ahead.

She got off the road immediately—not because she expected danger, but because she wanted to think about what to do next, and leaving herself anywhere she might be spotted might well take the choice out of her hands. The smoke was far enough away that unless the people behind it were posting a *very* thorough cordon of guards, they wouldn't have spotted her yet. But that would change pretty fast if she continued on the way she had been.

Strike out overland again, or keep to the road? She chewed on her lower lip, considering. The first option was the sensible one. The second was more interesting.

"Probably just some charcoal burner," she muttered to herself. "Or a hunter." Leopard hides fetched a good price in the lowlands.

Or it could be something Aadet would want to know about.

Ree grinned. *Sure, blame Aadet's curiosity. It isn't your own talking, not at all.*

She took a moment to make sure she was as masked as she could get, dulling her clothing down to a drab green and brown that would blend in well with the surrounding forest, and tucking the loose ends of her sash into the band so she could at least minimize the flash of red. Then she struck out through the trees, trying to find a vantage point that would let her spy on the fire from above.

It turned out to be coming from the edge of the road—not a place anybody would choose if they wanted secrecy. She couldn't get close enough to see without crossing to the other side, though, where the ground rose into a small ridge. Ree was contemplating whether to risk the open air when a voice from behind her said, "*Ra stavit kaz.*"

She cursed under her breath, but made no attempt to draw her sabre. Anybody who wanted her dead wouldn't have bothered to announce himself before striking. Instead she held her hands up, showing they were empty, and rose from her crouch to see who had caught her.

Embarrassingly, it was a pair of striplings, not more than sixteen, armed with flintlock pistols they didn't look ready to use. "You're good," Ree said in Solaine, testing. They weren't local; that much was obvious. Their skin was too light a brown, a shade lighter than her own, and they wore wide belts over shirts with rolled-up sleeves that hadn't been designed with this climate in mind. But they might still have spoken the local tongue.

They might have—but they didn't. The shorter of the two snapped a few questions at her, all in that same unfamiliar language. Ree could guess at their meaning well enough: *Who are you? What are you doing here?* "I mean you no harm," she said, this time in Japil, the most common trade tongue in the region. That got a flicker of recognition. The taller youth, who despite his height looked younger than his companion, said haltingly, "Others are where?"

"No others," Ree said. "I'm alone. Just a traveler."

A hurried conference between the two boys in their own language. Conferring about what to do with her, no doubt. Then the taller one said, "Me you give your sword."

"Like hell," Ree muttered under her breath. Anybody who tried to take that blade from her was going to lose a hand in the attempt.

But she didn't want to start bloodshed if she could avoid it. Moving slowly, she reached behind her head and brought her braid forward. They frowned. She untied the leather thong from its tail, then used that to tie her sabre's hilt to its sheath. The thong was pretty worn out; she could snap it with one good yank if she needed to. And depending on what these boys had in mind, she might need to.

A memory flickered up from the depths. Once upon a time, she'd known how to tie a knot that would look good to most people, but would unravel at a single tug. But she didn't remember it now, and couldn't exactly experiment in front of these two. *Something to work on later.*

For now, this satisfied the boys, at least enough to be going on with. "With us you come," the taller one said. The other gestured with his flintlock, indicating she should go first.

Together they climbed to the road, Ree contemplating

her options. The boys were good at stealth, but not at escorting prisoners. She could certainly take out one. The other might shoot her in the process, but the flintlocks were single-shot; unless he hit something vital, she'd still be on her feet. But the sound might bring others, and then she'd be running, probably wounded, with an unknown number of people on her tail. Over rough terrain, where there were leopards. Would that be better or worse than walking blind into whatever lay ahead?

She reminded herself that the fire was at the edge of the road. This wasn't a military camp. Civilians might be just as hostile, but she should at least give them a chance to prove otherwise before she killed anyone.

Civilians or not, they were keeping a good watch. Before she and her escorts got within sight of the fire, they were challenged from cover by another voice. The shorter boy responded, presumably recounting how they'd found her. Ree's skin crawled until she spotted the lookout, who had the good sense to perch himself in a tree. He had a long gun, but he wasn't aiming it at her. *Good.*

They went onward, around a curve in the track, and she found herself on the edge of a small caravan.

The carts and wagons hadn't stopped haphazardly, but they hadn't made an encampment either. Instead they were drawn up in a defensive huddle, except for one off to the side. That turned out to be the reason for the fire. The wagon had rolled too close to the edge of the road and ground up against a stone, damaging its wheel. A blacksmith had set up in the open air, well away from anything he didn't want to burn, and was preparing to hammer the rim back into alignment. Until that was done, these people weren't going anywhere.

And they weren't happy about it. Travelers delayed by a broken wheel usually took the opportunity to relax, stretching their legs if they'd been riding or getting off their feet if they'd been walking. They took naps or busied themselves with useful tasks. The people here just waited, watching in all directions, and the youths carrying babes in arms tried to hush them the moment they cried—as if the blacksmith's hammer wouldn't make as much noise as any infant.

Ree's arrival was like kicking an anthill. Those with small children recoiled to safety in the wagons or under the awnings spread alongside them, while the adults stepped forward to shield their young. Ree put her hands up again, empty and spread, making herself as nonthreatening as she could. They didn't look reassured; *Probably because I've got a sword on my hip.* Well, too bad—she still wasn't giving it up, not even for their peace of mind. Especially not when she didn't know who they were, or what they were doing there.

Her escorts called out an explanation, in the stifled voices of boys who didn't quite dare shout. A teenaged girl took off, presumably to find the leader of this traveling band. She didn't have to go far. Before Ree could do more than wonder if she'd seen people like these before, two more approached: a man and a woman in their forties or fifties, with large silver spools stretching their earlobes, like marks of rank. Their knee-length coats were profoundly unsuited to this heat, but made them look more official than shirtsleeves would have, and people stepped back to let them through.

The woman spoke first, in accented Japil. "Who are you?"

"My name is Ree. I mean your people no harm."

The woman's gaze flicked up and down, noting the sabre still on Ree's hip. Her lips tightened fractionally: no doubt the boys would be getting a lecture about that later. Then, not taking her eyes off Ree, she bent toward the man at her side and murmured in his ear. *Translator,* Ree assumed. *And his wife? I think so.* Ree wished she could risk working on their language, but that would give away far more than she dared right now.

The woman didn't wait for the man to say anything. Her next question, like the first, was her own. "Why are you on this road?"

"I'm on my way to Taraspai."

It was the wrong answer. Ree had been gambling on these people being foreigners; they weren't Solaine or Uyel, the people to the north, and she'd assumed they didn't know the local geography very well. But the woman frowned and snapped, "This isn't the road to Taraspai."

"I know," Ree said, suppressing the urge to curse. "I came through the mountains, from the north." What could she say that wouldn't sound insane? "I . . . wanted to avoid notice."

They would assume she had a pack somewhere, or maybe a donkey to carry things for her. The only reason to avoid notice on her way through the mountains was if she were a smuggler—or at least, that would be the only reason they would think of. Ree hoped.

Did that make these people smugglers? There was no bloody reason for them to be on this road. They couldn't have cut through the mountains like she had, not with those wagons in tow. They weren't miners, headed off to reopen one of the old quarries. But what kind of smugglers would bring along so many kids?

At least the delay imposed by translation gave her time to think, and to be ready for the next question. "Why were you following us?"

"I wasn't. I saw smoke, and I wanted to make sure it wasn't coming from anything I needed to be worried about. Then your boys caught me and brought me here. If they'd left me alone, I would be well past you by now. I'm happy to get back to doing that, just as soon as you let me go."

The woman spat on the ground. "And then you will go and tell the others about us. So they can finish what they started!"

"Zhutore." The voice came from behind Ree, off to the left. She twisted in time to see a man standing in the shade of a nearby tree.

Had she seen him in the light, she would have missed it; the effect was fading as he came forward. But in the shade, she caught glimmers of red along his neck and bare arms, following the tracery of his veins.

Well, shit.

Lightning sparked through Ree's own veins, but she kept her expression neutral. Just because she'd identified him didn't mean he'd done the same to her. Apart from the sash and the sabre, and a pendant of cool ember hidden under her shirt, there was nothing to identify her as an archon—not so long as she kept herself masked. And until she had some idea of his nature, she wasn't about to reveal herself.

His appearance didn't give much away. Once the red light had faded, he looked almost ordinary. He wasn't exceptionally tall or short, and his coloration wasn't much different from the people around him—a bit darker of skin and hair, but that was it. No claws or wings or extra arms. His build was compact, strong without being impressive. The densely embroidered strip of fabric that formed a diamond-shaped drape across his chest and back was a work of art, and Ree suspected it was one of his icons. Otherwise he wouldn't be wearing it while traveling along a dusty road, any more than she would be wearing a blood-red sash while sneaking through the forest.

He stopped a short distance away and addressed Zhutore in their own tongue. Ree itched to know what they were saying—but even if she unmasked, learning would take too long to be any use to her right now. The sound of it was nigglingly familiar, though. She listened as Zhutore's husband responded, and tried to remember when she'd heard the language before. Their clothing was vaguely familiar, too. And the carts and wagons they traveled in . . . a whole population, not just adults but a host of children, like an entire village on the move. Refugees?

No, not exactly. "You're Korenat, aren't you."

It stopped the conversation dead. Even those who didn't understand the trade tongue would have been able to pick out the name of their own people, and Zhutore glared pure murder as if Ree had uncovered some vital secret. The archon only looked interested. "Yes, we are.

Of the Nevati Korenat. Well, Zhutore and the others are. Have you met our kind before?"

"I've heard stories." And probably met them in previous lives, though none of those memories had come back to her yet. There were Korenat all over the world—anywhere they hadn't been run out of with fire and blades. Wanderers, but not by choice; the stories gave a half-dozen reasons for their nomadic existence, ranging from a homeland sunk into the sea to an ancient curse that forbade them to go home. Mostly, though, they moved around because the lands they traveled through didn't want them to stay. Even when local laws permitted them to settle down, they made good scapegoats any time there was a plague or other disaster.

And disaster might explain why they were in the middle of nowhere. Ree took another look around, more carefully this time. She found scars on the sides of wagons, as if they'd been struck with blades, and bandages on a number of the Korenat. Fresh ones—not more than a day or two old. Whatever trouble they ran afoul of, it had found them here in the mountains.

Ree said, "I didn't realize there was a Korenat settlement in Solaike." She'd been gone for nearly a year; that wasn't much time for them to establish themselves here. Didn't mean they hadn't, though.

But the archon said, "There isn't. At least, not yet. We

heard that the situation had changed here, and we hoped the new king would permit us to settle."

He still sounded optimistic, which meant their injuries weren't the result of any official attempt to drive them out. "So who attacked you?"

Zhutore had subsided, translating the conversation for her husband, but letting the unnamed archon do the talking. He said, "I don't know. We came by the main road, and the guards at the border permitted us to pass—but then we were ambushed."

Ambushed? Ree swore inwardly. Nearly a year: it was more than enough time for the political situation here to take a turn for the worse. Had the king been overthrown? No, she would have heard about that, in Uytan if nowhere else.

"Can you describe the ambushers?" she asked. "Were they Solaine? Did they wear armor?"

The man she thought was Zhutore's husband answered her questions, through his wife. "We believe they were Solaine, yes, but not soldiers. Their armor was good, but it did not match."

Neither did the armor of the king's people, last time Ree had seen them. Outfitting everyone properly took a while, after a generation of guerrilla warfare in the mountains. "Were they wearing leopard pelts, or did they have leopard patterns painted on their gear?"

The word "leopard" defeated Zhutore's ability to translate. "Spots," Ree said. She spat on her finger and knelt, using the wet tip to mark rosettes on one of the stones of the road. "Fur or paint."

"Paint, yes. In red."

"In *red*?" That wasn't any insignia Ree knew. Had the king created a new unit? But no, they'd said the border guards let them pass. Unless the left hand was seriously failing to talk to the right, that shouldn't have happened. "The soldiers at the border—were they the same?"

"No, their armor was painted in yellow and black."

She started to ask why the Korenat hadn't gone back to the border after the attack, but swallowed the question. Assaulted by strangers, in a land they didn't know ... they had no reason to think the guards would help them. "You know you're headed away from the trade road, right?"

The archon shrugged helplessly. "The trade road was not safe. We lost six when they attacked us. We hoped this would lead us to a village, away from the ambushers."

"It's leading you from nowhere to nowhere." Ree stood up and wiped her fingertip on her breeches. "You've got to get back east, or you'll be stuck up here forever." But they couldn't risk the main road—not when they had no guarantee they wouldn't just be slaughtered. She closed her eyes, calling on the familiarity built up over two years of hiding with the revolutionaries. *We intercepted Saalik's strike force not far from here, didn't we?*

"Look," she said, glancing up and down the track. "Continue on the way you have been for a while longer—once you've got that wheel repaired. You'll come to a fork in the road, one bit leading onward and up, the other down. Follow the downward path. It isn't in good shape, and it'll look like it's taking you the wrong way, but it'll loop around and bring you to a farm village eventually. From there you can get back to the main road, but in more settled territory. It should be safe." She tried to sound confident, and mostly succeeded.

"Why should we trust you?" Zhutore demanded.

The archon said something to her in their own tongue. Zhutore looked less than entirely convinced, her jaw setting hard. Ree said, "Look, I don't care whether you follow my advice or not. But I promise you this much; I'll carry word down to the lowlands for you. The king will want to know there's somebody ambushing travelers on the trade road."

"Or you'll tell the attackers where we are. You wear their color." She pointed at Ree's sash.

And if I could have hidden it, I would have. "If I really wanted to do that, I would have killed your boys out in the forest and vanished, rather than letting them drag me back here."

"Zhutore." The archon spoke quietly, but it carried weight. The woman fell silent, and he said to Ree, "Please, join me. We cannot go anywhere until the wheel is repaired, so Zhutore will be satisfied, because you will not be able to tell anyone where we are until we are no longer there. And I will be satisfied, because I will have a chance to offer you hospitality, after this unfriendly welcome."

She eyed him warily. Was he *seimer* or *gemer*? Every archon had two aspects, one more or less creative, one destructive, but they manifested in different ways for different archai. *Seimer* wasn't always nice, and *gemer* wasn't always bad. Without knowing anything about this archon's story, she had no way of guessing what he might do.

"I don't even know your name," Ree said, stalling.

"Mevreš," he said. "Will you join me?"

That wasn't his true name, of course. He would never offer that up to a stranger—assuming he even knew it. "Ree" was just a piece of her true name, the only piece she remembered, and too small to be of use to anybody else. She ground her teeth, but his question was more in the nature of a command. Ree sighed and followed, keeping her hand from her blade.

Mevreš took her around the edge of the caravan, skirting the fire where the blacksmith was still working, and arrived at a wagon with an awning propped up along its side. He pulled out a small, padded bench, then began searching in the back of the wagon for something. Ree perched on the bench and tried to think of small talk.

She failed to come up with anything that didn't sound inane before Mevreš rejoined her, carrying a small bag the size of his two fists together. A girl-child of about nine ran up at the same time, carrying a leather-wrapped flask that turned out to contain boiling water. Mevreš poured this into two cups and began to whisk in a powder from the bag. The scent was rich and bitter, and Ree closed her eyes to hide the echoes it called up in her mind. She'd had that drink before, in another life. She could almost taste it on her tongue, but the memory kept slipping through her fingers.

"You don't have to mask yourself."

The words hit like a shock of cold water. Ree opened her eyes to find him offering one of the cups. She took it by reflex, eyeing him warily. He smiled, all friendliness. "I've been around for long enough to recognize my own kind. Even masked."

So much for hoping he hadn't identified her. Ree felt like she'd walked into some kind of trap, even though there was no reason to panic. If he wanted to gain an advantage over her, he would have been better off not saying anything, letting her think he didn't know.

Well, no point hiding now. "Is that why your veins were

glowing red?" Ree asked, and let her appearance shift.

Even unmasked, she could pass for human at a glance. She hadn't been around for long enough to acquire the distinctive features that tended to mark archai. Her eyes were too perfect a black, and left to its own devices, her clothing darkened to the same color; her sash was the only spot of brightness, and a few touches of silver on the leather vambraces that held her sleeves close against her forearms. But a mortal who didn't know much about archai would just think she was foreign—which she was, everywhere she went—or had strange taste in clothing.

Mevreš laughed at her question. "You saw that, did you? No, I don't need to show myself to spot an archon. After a while, you just learn to tell."

A wisp of smoke rose from his lips on the final words, curling too perfectly in the air to be natural. He'd dropped his own mask again as he spoke, and now the differences that marked him as an archon were visible. Ree openly studied his veins, where they showed past the collar and the sleeveless edges of his vest. They didn't precisely flow; it was more of a shifting metallic glitter, only visible in dim light, or from the right angle. His hair was black, but it held a red highlight the same shade as his veins. And he was less human-looking than she'd thought, though apart from the smoke it was hard to put her finger on any single detail that marked him. He managed to radiate an intense familiarity, as if she ought to know him, even though her memory insisted that she didn't.

"How long have you been in the world?" she asked, curious.

"Oh, I don't know. I stopped counting ages ago. Fifty years? Sixty?"

She almost dropped her cup. A spill would have hurt; the liquid inside was still too hot to drink, more than hot enough to scald. "You've been bound for fifty or sixty years?"

"Not at all," Mevreš said. "The Korenat woman who summoned me freed me after less than a year. Once she realized that I came from her people."

This time Ree decided to put the cup down until it was cool enough to drink, or Mevreš stopped saying things that made her want to drop it. It wasn't unheard of for an archon to find their way back to their place of origin, the people who first told the story from which they sprang—assuming those people even still existed, so many ages later. The world was littered with the relics of lost kingdoms and empires.

But even getting a chance to return home was damned rare. There was no guarantee that anybody who tried to summon an archon out of the apeiron would get one from the tales of their own land, instead of a creature from the other side of the world; summoners skilled enough to be that precise were vanishingly rare. Ree herself had started this lifetime in a country called Tábh Rig, and wherever she was from, it sure as hell wasn't there.

And starting out in the wrong country was just the beginning of the challenge. Humans only summoned and bound archai when they had some problem that needed solving, something beyond their own mortal abilities. When that problem was gone . . . most of the time they dismissed the archon, sending them back to the realm of non-existence they came from.

"Dismissed" being a polite way of saying "murdered."

"What about you?" Mevreš asked. "Did your summoner free you?"

It happened sometimes, but not often. "No," Ree said. "I broke free on my own. You've been with these people that whole time?" She thought, but didn't say, *When you could have gone anywhere?*

"Not with this *koton*, no. I visit many groups of Korenat—as many as I can."

She remembered him saying that Zhutore and the others were Nevati Korenat, implying that he himself wasn't. Now it made sense: Korenat, but not of this particular group. He'd found his people . . . but they were everywhere, scattered all over the world. The thought made her ache inside. "So what are you, then? Some kind of guardian?"

Mevreš eyed her narrowly over his cup. He'd already taken a sip from it; maybe his nature made him immune to burning his tongue. "You haven't spoken to many archai, have you."

"I try to avoid it." *Ever since the first archon I met in this life stole something from me.* No, that wasn't fair; Ree had traded it away, of her own free will. She just didn't get to choose what she gave up, or even know what it had been.

He nodded, unsurprised. "Inasmuch as we can be said to have any kind of society amongst ourselves, we don't generally ask one another so bluntly. To know another archon's story is, in a way, a kind of power."

Because archai were bound by the rules of their individual natures. If Mevreš's story was that of a guardian to his people, Ree could manipulate him by threatening the Korenat; he would feel compelled to protect them. If he was some kind of peacemaker, Ree could cut him down where he sat, and he might not even be able to fight back. If he was a trickster, all bets were off. She would find out his nature eventually—after so much time in the world, he was so intensely attuned to it that he couldn't even think of going against it—but she understood not volunteering that information to someone he'd met only a few minutes ago.

"Do you not like your drink?" Mevreš asked, before she could decide whether she wanted to apologize or not.

Ree picked up her cup and blew on its contents until it seemed cool enough to risk. The liquid burned in more than one way; there were spices in that powder, mixed with a bitter base. It shouldn't have tasted as good as it did. "I think I've had this before—in another lifetime."

"Do you remember its meaning?"

She froze. Mevreš smiled—more of an apologetic grimace. "I'm afraid I tricked you, but only for my people's protection. Now that we've shared *šokol*, I will not offer violence to you, and you will not offer violence to me. At least not before the sun sets—and I hope not after."

Bastard. A masked archon was little better than a human; the price of concealing their nature was that they couldn't draw on its strengths, either. But Mevreš had been in the world for decades, remembering his past, rebuilding his power. And this, it seemed, was one of the things he could do . . . so long as he unmasked first.

Ree thought about throwing the cup in his face, and couldn't tell whether she didn't because she wasn't actually that angry, or because his prohibition against violence stopped her from doing it.

"I don't know you," he said, by way of explanation. "But you walk armed, and we've suffered enough losses already. I couldn't risk it."

She put the *šokol* back down. Her taste for it was gone. "I gave you advice. And I promised to carry word of the attack to the king's court."

"I had the strong impression you only did that in the hopes of getting away from us."

"Well, yes—but that doesn't mean I was lying."

"What good would it do us for you to tell people in the lowlands there are outlaws up here? They won't send soldiers to rescue a Korenat caravan. They have no reason to care what happens to us."

"Then what do you want from me?"

Mevreš leaned forward, his gaze intense. "You know these mountains. We don't. We fled Hezâre because there was sickness there, and when that kind of thing happens, Korenat make a convenient target. Uytan wouldn't let us stay; their council would only let us pass through their territory, for fear we carried the sickness. Which, I assure you, we do not. So we came into Solaike—but the first thing we encountered here was an ambush. We cannot assume that our luck will improve. My people could die up here; we don't have enough food to survive in this kind of wilderness. We need more than advice on which path to take; we need a guide. And you're the best hope we have."

Ree stared at him. "Me. Your best hope. A complete stranger, an archon who walks around armed. Someone you trust so little, you decided to spiritually bind her not to attack you."

He spread his hands. "Take a look around. Study our other hopes, and then tell me which one surpasses you."

She didn't have to look around. She knew the region, and she'd seen their caravan. Children, wounded adults, carts and wagons not meant for this terrain. They had no better hope. Except to wander along these mountain paths, praying they wouldn't take a wrong turn in a landscape that had twenty of those for every right one. They'd find their way out eventually, she imagined . . . but not before they lost more people to starvation, predators, and accidents.

Ree gritted her teeth. She didn't like knowing that Mevreš had trapped her in this position—but she also didn't like the idea of just abandoning these people. "If I help you, what do I get in return?"

He raised an ironic eyebrow. "You won't do it out of the goodness of your heart?"

"Seeing into people's hearts is clearly not your gift."

His laugh was heartier than the joke deserved, but it released a little of the tension that had built up. "Very well. I offer you stories."

Did he have some way of seeing into her soul after all? It was better bait than it should have been, but she hid her reaction. "Stories don't get me very far."

"You haven't been in the world very long, have you? I have—long enough to remember a great many of my previous lives. I have been to lands all over the world, whether summoned by humans or traveling with the Korenat. If I share those stories, they may spark memories that would be of use to you."

Ree's jaw tensed. An archon had offered her a similar deal once, at the very beginning of this lifetime. But Mevreš was not the Lhian, and this was not the trap that had been. The Lhian had offered Ree her *own* stories—knowledge of her own past, her true nature. For the archai, memories were power, the path to regaining their strength and gifts. But if Ree had taken the Lhian's bait, she would have put herself into the other archon's control, probably forever. All Mevreš wanted was a guide out of the mountains.

Assuming Ree believed him.

"Mask," she said, "and then offer that deal again."

He did as she ordered. It wasn't a guarantee—there were no guarantees, when dealing with an archon—but at the very least he wasn't using any hidden gifts to sway her mind while he said it.

"Fine," Ree said. "I'll get you out of the mountains. Now, while your blacksmith finishes with that wheel, start talking."

• • •

Mevreš was as good as his word, and a splendid story-teller. It took them three days to get out of the mountains, five to reach the capital of Taraspai, and he talked the whole way, except when Ree told him to shut up. Which she only did when they needed silence, because his stories fed a hunger deep inside her.

It wasn't even that his voice carried any particular power, at least not that she could tell. The smoke that occasionally rose with his breath wasn't drugged or anything like that. Mevreš, she thought, just enjoyed talking. He told her about the places he'd been, in this lifetime and ones previous, until she started to think there was no corner of the world he hadn't visited. At one point Ree almost asked if he'd ever encountered an archon called the Lhian, but she closed her mouth before the words came out. If she asked that, she would wind up telling her own story—the tale of how she encountered the Lhian, and the deal she'd struck. She wasn't ready to admit that to a near stranger, however friendly he might be.

But the stories he told called up echoes in her mind. Distant ones for the most part, as if he'd struck one bell in a carillon, and the others all hummed in response. Not enough to trigger the kind of memory cascade she hoped for. But every so often something else clicked and she knew she'd been to that city before, or known someone with a similar habit. She hoarded those moments like treasures, fitting them in among the few shreds of memory she'd regained since leaving the Lhian's island. Archai came out of the apeiron with nothing but the instincts of their own natures, no recollection of the lives that had gone before. Every fragment Mevreš gave her was precious.

It was more than payment enough for her efforts.

But she didn't spend the entire time with him. Even if she'd wanted to, she couldn't have avoided the women of the Nevati Korenat. They were the traders of their people, which explained why Zhutore had been playing interpreter; they spoke assorted trade tongues with varying degrees of skill. Every last one of them wanted to know what Ree could tell them about Taraspai and Solaike in general: how much certain goods usually cost in local coin, how far people here expected to bargain up or down, how to be polite and how to spot rudeness. It was survival work, a counterpart to the work the men did hunting game and keeping watch over the caravan at night. If they were going to live in Solaike, they needed to know the rules for getting by.

"Why do you want to settle down here?" Ree asked Zhutore, the night after they got out of the mountains. "You barely know anything about this place."

Zhutore's hostility had faded by slow degrees. She still wasn't friendly, but Ree suspected the number of people

Zhutore called "friend" would fit on one hand with fingers to spare. She said, "What other choice do we have? We lived in Hezâre for more than a generation, but when the plague came—" The flick of her hand spoke volumes. "We had to go somewhere. Here things are unsettled, but sometimes that means opportunity. And it's bad enough for the children, losing the only home they ever knew; we don't want them to live through the hardship of wandering."

They sat in silence for a moment, studying the embers of the fire over which Zhutore's daughter had cooked their meal. Then Zhutore asked bluntly, "Do you think we'll be allowed to stay?"

Ree traced her fingertips along the lines worked into her vambraces. She hadn't bothered masking again after her first conversation with Mevreš; everybody in the *koton* knew she was an archon, and there were benefits to not hiding her nature. "I don't know. I come and go from Solaike; I was here off and on during the days of the revolution, and then less often since then. I don't know what the current political situation is."

"But you know people here. Important people."

That had come out when Ree talked about the mountains, that she'd been among the rebels. Many of those who had survived the fighting were now officials in the new government. "Some. One of the king's wives in particular."

"Will you speak on our behalf to these people?"

She'd been expecting that question for the last day; the only surprise was that Zhutore hadn't waited a little longer before asking it. It wasn't just the way the women kept coming to her for advice; Mevreš had been introducing her to individuals all over the caravan, from old Granny Nivmi to a passel of children. Turning strangers into, if not friends, then at least *people*. People with names and personalities and families. If Mevreš could make Ree care about them in the few days he had to work with, then by all the higher powers, he was going to do it.

Guiding them out of the mountains was the least of the favors he wanted from her.

"I'll tell the king's wife about how you were attacked," she said, guarded. Then, after a pause: "I'll ask if he's willing to help you. But no promises."

Zhutore looked puzzled. "He?"

She clearly thought Ree had misspoken. Ree grinned. "You'll see."

• • •

Parts of Taraspai had burned during the revolution, and the scars were still there. The Great Bazaar that stood midway between the city's edge and the palace had been rebuilt, but only recently; the building stood out sharply, the wood of its roof beams too new among the older structures surrounding it, some of which showed scorch marks or obvious repairs. Many of the streetside shrines were still broken and defaced: one of the greatest upheavals Valtaja introduced was the attempted overthrow of the old religion, exalting the soldiers' fire god alone above all others. In the end, that turned out to be his greatest mistake.

Two Korenat riding through the city on their way to the palace compound didn't attract much attention; there were foreigners aplenty in the city, with the king aggressively pursuing alliances and connections with neighboring lands after Valtaja's long isolation. But Ree wasn't masked, and although very few ordinary citizens knew about her, the black of her clothes and the red of her sash made her a noticeable figure in the streets.

Guards halted them at the front gate of the palace, beneath the towering mud-brick walls. It wasn't one of the king's audience days, or they would have had to fight their way through a crowd to get anywhere near the gate. But even on an ordinary day, a line of people waited to deliver messages or request permission to speak with someone else in the compound. "How long will we have to wait?" Zhutore asked.

"I'm guessing about—" Even the brief estimate Ree intended to make was too long. One of the guards spotted her, and his eyes widened. Maybe not everybody in Taraspai could recognize her, but *that* guy definitely could. Ree strode past the waiting petitioners and said, "Aadet Temini."

"Of course," the guard stammered, and beckoned to one of the flock of messenger-children waiting by the gate.

They still had to wait, because finding anybody in the palace compound was often a lengthy process. But all things considered, it wasn't very long before the messenger came back and escorted them through the palace gardens to the house Aadet occupied with some of the king's other male wives.

Ree still stumbled a bit over thinking of him that way. In this place, "wife" was a political term, not a familial one; kingship in Solaike was an extension of the lineages that bound the country together, and Aadet's "marriage" was a way of joining him to the royal household, which doubled as the government. Even most of the king's female wives weren't his spouses in the usual sense—just a pack of women who served as officials in various capacities, mediating between the lineages of their birth and the one they'd married into.

Even so, Aadet's new status meant certain changes. Gone was the leather vest he'd worn on the Lhian's island, replaced by a much finer one decorated with colorful stitching. His hair was braided along his scalp in a geometric pattern, and a touch of gold dust on his eyelids signaled his rank.

For Ree, though, the biggest difference was an invisible one, marked by what Aadet didn't do, instead of what he did. When they were fighting at each other's sides in the mountains, he would have greeted her with a strong embrace, clapping her on the back like a fellow soldier. They'd shared a bedroll back then, and sometimes more than that. But to touch the king's wife, whether male or female, was not permitted.

Instead he laid one hand over his heart, grinning broadly. "Every time you leave, I wonder if I'll see you again."

"Afraid I'll die, or just that I'll forget the road here?"

He snorted. The physical distance between them might have grown, but they were still close in other ways. Formality didn't count much between them. "You don't forget the road anywhere. No, I'm just worried you'll decide you've had enough of this place, and show us your heels for good."

"I've certainly had enough of your summers," Ree said wryly. The heat wasn't the issue, of course, and they both knew it. The revolution was over; in its place came politics, the delicate business of rebuilding a country, and Ree didn't have the inclination or the talent for that. Neither did Aadet, if they were being honest—but they never were. Not out loud. He'd sworn himself to the man who was now his king, and couldn't walk away just because the fun part was over.

They bantered to avoid talking about that, or about Ree's own frequent and lengthy absences from Solaike. Even during the revolution she'd come and gone, throwing herself full tilt into their fight while she was around, but then leaving them to it for weeks or months at a time. Aadet wanted her to stay . . . but she couldn't, and he knew it.

He even knew most of the reasons why.

She still found an open door every time she came back, though. Their friendship was good enough for that much. And, Ree hoped, for assistance.

Aadet looked curiously at the two Korenat. "You've brought friends with you."

"Zhutore Iv Vlaya Nevaten and her husband, Rovit Šek Taça Nevaten," Ree said. She'd coached the two of them for this moment; they greeted Aadet in accented but comprehensible Solaine and touched their hearts in the formal manner, with both hands. Then Ree said, "They ran into a welcoming party on their way out of the mountains. Let's sit down, and I'll tell you about it."

They could have told their own story; Aadet spoke Japil well enough to understand the gist of it. But

Zhutore and Rovit had guessed, rightly, that it would carry more weight in Aadet's native tongue . . . and that Ree, as his friend, could command more of his attention than a pair of strangers ever would.

She delivered the tale with almost the concision of a report, knowing that for something like this, Aadet wouldn't have much patience with the slow buildup of detail and tension. But she gave him the names of all the Nevati who had died, and the litany of the wounded, because the point wasn't just to alert Aadet to a military threat; she was here for the Korenat, to help them gain acceptance in the Solaine court. They would need palace backing for that to happen, the support of at least one of the king's high-ranking female wives, and if Ree could get Aadet's sympathy, they'd be halfway there.

He listened with increasing grimness. When Ree was done, he muttered, "The Red Leopard." She raised an eyebrow; he saw it and said, "Remnants of Valtaja's army."

Strictly speaking, the army those remnants came from had ultimately belonged to Valtaja's son and successor, who lost the staff to Enkettsivaane, the new king. But everyone still spoke of his father instead, the man who seized control from the previous royal lineage and brought Solaike to its knees. Even more than seven years dead, Valtaja cast a long shadow—one it seemed they hadn't yet managed to eradicate. "Who's leading them?" Ree asked.

"Sihpo Teglane," Aadet said. "Valtaja's nephew. Not the military genius his uncle was, but he's smart enough to know he can't oust Enkettsivaane in a direct attack. So instead he'll make the royal lineage unpopular, destroy the stability we're trying to build, until enough people hate us that they'll be willing to support a new claimant."

"And so they're disrupting trade. If the king can't protect even the main road, the effects of that will ripple outward pretty fast." The major lineages of Solaike were all trading families, and the smaller bloodlines who were clients to them depended heavily on the money and goods their patrons brought in.

Aadet nodded. Then he rubbed at his brow and spoke in Japil, addressing Zhutore and Rovit. "Words can't make up for what you've lost, but you have my sincere apologies. It's the responsibility of the palace to make the roads in this kingdom safe, and we've failed you. I'll arrange some kind of compensation—it's the best I can do."

Knowing Aadet, the compensation would come out of his own wealth. The kinds of trade a king's wife was allowed to engage in were limited, but he wasn't wholly dependent on the royal household to support himself. Which was a good thing, since influence in the palace frequently depended on one of two things: wealth, and the ability to produce a potential heir to the royal staff.

"Money's good," Ree said, "but help is better. They're hoping to settle down in Solaike, not just pass through. You could speak for them to the king's ministers."

Aadet obviously hadn't yet thought that far, beyond the pleasant surprise of Ree's arrival and the unpleasant one of the Red Leopard's attack. He blinked, gaze drifting out of focus as he thought it through. He wasn't the most politically adept of the king's followers; Ree hoped his revolutionary past still carried some weight at the palace. Enkettsivaane owed his staff to Aadet, who had traveled halfway around the world and the rest of the way back home to bring him the words that would inspire the people of Solaike to his side. But the give-and-take of favors and gifts that drove palace decisions . . . finding his way across the treacherous island of the Lhian was easier for him than navigating the world he now lived in.

He questioned the two Korenat for a time, sounding them out on what they hoped to achieve and what they could offer his land in return. Their trades were portable ones; their ambitions were modest. *Basically they want to be able to live here and not get killed, enslaved, or taxed into starvation,* Ree thought. It didn't sound like much to ask—but she was even worse at palace games than Aadet was. A king still trying to consolidate his power might see a pack of Korenat refugees as an unnecessary disruption.

"I'll see what I can do," Aadet said at last. From his tone, Ree knew what would come next. He was going to ask her to help.

He'd forgotten what day it was.

She couldn't really blame him. If she didn't stay in Solaike, he couldn't be expected to keep track. But even as he turned to face her, she shook her head. "I'll be out of the city for a few days," she said. "I'll check back in after I return, see where things stand."

Aadet shut his mouth. Zhutore looked at Ree, plainly curious; she might not be able to hear their unspoken conversation, but she wasn't blind enough to miss that there had been one. "Thank Mevreš again for the stories," Ree said to her, and left.

• • •

Whether Zhutore passed along the message or not, Ree never found out. But when she came back into the city three days later, it took Mevreš less than a day to show up on her doorstep.

She spent most of the intervening time at the palace. Aadet's first words to her upon her return were, "We're going after the Red Leopard. Want to come along?"

Ree grinned. "You even have to ask?"

The rebels against Enkettsivaane had been busy. The Korenat weren't the first ones they'd attacked, but nobody else had survived to report before that; in the days since, more stories had filtered down to the capital, of merchants killed and caravans burnt. Ree looked at the list of incidents and shook her head. "Either they're way the hell more numerous than they should be, or they're driving themselves *really* hard right now."

"Probably the latter," Aadet said. He grimaced. "I *hope* the latter. It makes sense—hit hard and fast right out of the gate, when people don't know yet to be extra wary. Once word gets out, merchants will hire more guards, and then these strikes will get more difficult. But the more damage they do now, the more frightened people will be afterward, even if the attacks get less frequent. They'll be able to ride that reputation for a good long while."

Unless the king's forces could crush them, and fast. "How soon do you plan to leave?"

"As soon as we can get out the door," Aadet said. "Which should have been three days ago, if it weren't for the politics of it."

With her, he didn't even try to hide his frustration. The problem wasn't getting the king's ministers and officials to agree on action against the Red Leopard; it was deciding who should lead the counterattack. Every influential lineage in Solaike wanted to provide the commander—even those who were never a part of the revolutionary band in the mountains. *Especially* those who hadn't been. "Powers have pity," Ree said in disgust. "What the hell do the Tehiiga think they're going to do up there? Wander around in circles waiting for the Red Leopard to present themselves for smiting? They couldn't find their own asses in a forest without a native guide to lead them."

"If you think that's bad," Aadet said, "wait until you get to the part where you start wondering if they're secretly in league with the rebels, and only want to lead the expedition to make sure we get slaughtered." When Ree stared at him, his mouth twisted in a sour line. "Welcome to life in Solaike these days."

He wasn't joking. Somebody was funding Sihpo Teglane's efforts against the king; his rebels wouldn't have lasted this long without support. That someone might well be inside the palace. Ree started a mental list of possible suspects, then gave it up when she got a headache. There were too many lineages who might gain power if they supported a new royal line, or people within those lineages who could take over from the current heads under the right circumstances. Once she added in the possibility of providing wives to a new king—the kind who might give him an heir, with all the influence and benefits that brought—the list encompassed about ninety percent of Solaike's nobility.

Compared to the aftermath, winning a revolution was easy.

Those intrigues put Ree in a bad enough mood that she almost threw Mevreš out of the palace when he found her in one of the lesser gardens, where she was cleaning her boots. "How did you get in here?" she demanded, not pausing in her task. *Why can I mask these boots to look like anything I want, but I can't mask the mud on them?*

"I asked the guards to let me through," he said mildly.

"You're a damned archon." But he was masked, an ordinary-looking Korenat man, and she kept her voice low as she said it. If the palace guards didn't know he wasn't human, she didn't want to deal with the consequences of announcing it to the world.

His reply was equally quiet. "They don't know that. And before you start describing all the problems with me keeping it secret—I don't intend to be here for much longer. Either the Nevati will be allowed to stay, and I'll move on to another caravan, or they'll be told to leave, and I'll travel with them. Revealing myself now seems like opening everyone up to unnecessary trouble."

"You'll get a whole lot of necessary trouble if they find out the hard way." But Ree wasn't in any hurry to tell anybody. The ban against archai in Solaike had ended with Enkettsivaane's ascension—and she'd ignored it plenty herself, in the two years before that ascension—but the new government of Solaike hadn't decided yet how to deal with their kind. If Mevreš got caught, it would be on both of their heads; nobody would believe Ree hadn't known about him. But if he was leaving soon, she'd just as soon avoid the problem.

Ree studied him out of the corner of her eye, brushing the side of one boot with quick strokes. "Is that why you came to visit me? To make sure I'm keeping your secret?"

She expected confession, or false bluster that he intended nothing of the sort, or a graceful segue to the favor he really wanted to ask. She didn't expect him to deflate, as if somebody had promised him a song, and she refused to sing. "No. No, I trust you."

It was a substantial improvement over their first meeting, when he spiritually bound her not to hurt him. But the change had happened too fast. "You wanted me to speak for these Nevati to the king's people. I've done that. If you think I can manage anything more here, you're overestimating me by a long shot."

"It isn't that. I just—after all the stories I told. You drank *šokol*; you spent time with the women and the children . . . I thought, surely by now you would have figured it out."

Ree scowled and put down her brush. His sad, disappointed posture made her feel like a student failing to grasp an obvious lesson. It wasn't a pleasant feeling. Her voice was sharp as she said, "Let me guess. We knew each other in a past life."

"Quite possibly—though if we did, I haven't remembered it yet either. But no, I mean something much larger than that."

He kept searching her eyes as if he could look through them to see the light dawn inside. It didn't come; Ree had no idea what he was hinting at, and her attempts to figure it out weren't producing anything other than a growing desire to hit him. "Let's take it as given that I'm too thick to figure out what you mean, and get to the part where you tell me."

Mevreš said, "You're from the Korenat."

It should have been one of those moments where an intangible bell rang and memories flooded into her mind. If she came from the Korenat—if her spirit had its origin in stories told by Zhutore's ancestors, in the long-gone age when stories could come to life—surely Mevreš's words would have resonated in the core of her soul, just like the first time she heard the word "archon" and realized what she was.

But nothing came.

She'd met Korenat in previous lives; his stories had

called that much out of her memories. She remembered the taste of *šokol*, the sound of their language. But when she looked inside herself for a connection, she found nothing.

Less than nothing. Which made Mevreš's air of certainty all the more jarring. Ree picked up her brush again. "Sorry, but you're wrong."

"No, I'm not. This—this is what I do." He gestured with one hand at the opposite arm, at the veins that had glimmered red in the shade when he was unmasked. "I can *tell*. I suspected from the moment I saw you, just because of your appearance."

"I don't look much like Zhutore."

"Her skin is lighter than yours, it's true. The Nevati tend to be light skinned. They've traveled through too many lands, married out too many times over the centuries, for their appearance not to change. But there are Korenat in the world who look more like you. Some of them still wear sashes like yours." He waved these details away with an impatient hand. "But those were only reasons to suspect. I *know* when someone is Korenat, if I unmask. And you are."

Her boots weren't anything like clean, but Ree dropped the brush again and began tugging them back on anyway. "Then why don't I remember anything?"

Mevreš shook his head. "I don't know. Triggering

memories isn't a reliable process; maybe it's been too long since you met up with your own people—"

"You aren't my people." The words came out hard as steel, Ree on her feet and inches away from Mevreš's face. He held his ground, but not without flinching. "And if you decided I was Korenat the moment you laid eyes on me, why didn't you say anything before now?"

"Because it was clear that you *didn't* remember. How would you have reacted if I tried to claim a connection in our first meeting, when you barely even knew my name?"

In some ways it might have been better if he had. Ree would have laughed at him and assumed it was some feeble attempt at a trick. Instead she had this: days of friendliness, of stories shared in what she thought was good faith, and the entire time, Mevreš was fishing for something that wasn't there.

Even now, he believed it was true. He was waiting for the clouds to part, for Ree to fall silent and get a distant look in her eyes and then say, "Oh, powers, you're right; I remember now." But it was never going to happen. And the way he was looking at her—the wise elder patiently leading the child through the lesson—

"Get out of Solaike," she said. "You have until we go after the Red Leopard to move on, with or without the Nevati. If you're still here when that happens, I *will* expose you."

Then she stalked off through the garden, ramming her heels into the dirt as if to pound it into stone. But no amount of force jarring up through her body could erase the hollow, empty feeling in her gut.

. . .

In the end, by some political alchemy Ree didn't have the patience to identify, Aadet was chosen as the leader of the soldiers mustered against the Red Leopard. By naming one of his wives to the post, the king sent a message: although he was grateful to the various lineage heads for their support, he was asserting his own strength against those who would challenge it.

It meant that Aadet got to handpick the soldiers who would go into the mountains. Many of them were familiar to Ree, at least by sight; they were veterans of the revolution, men and women who had survived in the wilds during the years when they fought to take back their country. They knew that terrain inside and out . . . which wasn't the same thing as saying they knew every corner of it. "The truth is," Aadet said to Ree, "there are too many places for Sihpo's people to hide out there. More of them than even we know—and the real problem is, there are too many opportunities for them to move around. They might be in one of our old havens, but by the time we get there, they'll have shifted to their next base of operations."

It was what the revolutionaries used to do, and why they had succeeded for so many years at keeping themselves out of Valtaja's hands. There were at least a few among the new rebels who would remember that, and do their best to imitate it. "We've got one advantage over them, though," Ree said. "They don't know the land as well as you do. They won't move as fast, or as secretly. Sooner or later, we'll dig them out."

Aadet grimaced. "Oh, I'm sure. We just need it to be sooner, not later, because the longer they're out there, the worse it gets for us. If we can't dig them out quickly, we'll have to hope we at least keep them busy enough that they don't have much spare time to interfere with trade."

He pushed for them to leave as soon as possible, before the Red Leopard had more opportunities to strike. Even with Aadet's efforts, though, the expedition was delayed enough that Ree had to move out of the room she'd been given in the palace compound, finding temporary quarters in the city outside. She made sure he knew where she'd gone, and when a palace messenger boy found her there, she assumed Aadet had sent him to say it was time.

Instead he saluted and said, "There's a man who wants to meet with you, honored one. From those strangers—the Korenat. He said his name was Mevreš."

Ree had no idea what her expression looked like, but the boy immediately began to apologize. Ree waved that off. "Not your fault. Tell him . . ." Mevreš might just want to say goodbye. *And after that, all the little baby leopards will sprout wings and begin to fly.*

Well, if he started preaching her supposed Korenat past again, she could always walk away. After kicking him in the shins. If he had some other reason for arranging this meeting, she could give him at least a few minutes of her time. "Tell him I'll meet him outside the palace wall, on the southwest side. At noon." The boy saluted again, then scurried away.

Mevreš was already waiting when she arrived, well away from the dust and clamor of the gate market. She suspected he'd arrived early, just to be sure of not missing her. "I hope nothing is wrong," he said by way of greeting.

"Wrong?"

He nodded toward the wall, and the palace compound beyond. "You aren't lodging here anymore."

"I don't like spending too long in the palace," Ree said. Which was true, but incomplete. She wasn't eager to advertise her weaknesses, though, and the fact that she couldn't spend more than three nights in the same bed was one of them.

She'd tried various ways of cheating it, just as an

experiment—different beds in the same room, different corners of the room, different rooms in the same building—but fundamentally, it wasn't some game whose rules she could bend. It was just her nature as an archon, and so long as she knew she was looking for a loophole, there weren't any. She could have shifted to another room in the palace; Aadet would have made certain she got one. But it still would have made her chafe, and really, she didn't mind using the issue as an excuse to get clear of the palace. Aadet wasn't the only one who preferred being a revolutionary in the mountains to a politician in the city.

Mevreš let it pass, in favor of getting straight to the point. "You told me to leave. I would like to show you something first, and see what you think; it may be of use to your friends here. If, after seeing it, you tell me to reveal my true nature and offer my aid, I will do so. If you tell me to remain hidden, I will leave Solaike, as you asked."

It hadn't so much been a request as an order—but he had her curiosity up, and Ree knew he knew it. She crossed her arms and leaned against the palace wall. Its stones were already warm in the morning sun, cooking through her shirt into the muscles of her upper back. "Your aid. Against the Red Leopard?" He nodded. "Why?"

"Because it would help the Nevati."

Too pat. But challenging him on it would mean going back to their previous conversation, the one where he insisted she came from the Korenat. Ree preferred to let it pass. "So what help can you offer? Just because you're . . . what you are doesn't make you useful for everything. Who was that archon you told me about on the road—Mianglaia? Her story was that she was always in peril, always having to be rescued. Some help *she* would be in this."

Mevreš grinned. "She might be a great deal of help if the Red Leopard kidnapped her. Her rescuers never have any trouble finding their way to the dastardly villains who did the deed."

"Or she might be threatened by an actual leopard, which wouldn't do us any good at all. And whatever your story is, I know you're not a maiden waiting for rescue. What good do you think you can do us, out there? You couldn't even find your own way out of the mountains."

The bluntness got to him; she could see his shoulders twitch, the little flinch of vulnerability. "I may not be able to find the rebels," Mevreš said. "But I might be able to find answers."

"What do you mean?"

"You don't remember much about the Korenat—" Before Ree could say anything, he put up one conciliatory hand. "This is not about you. I only mean that you may not recall one of the means by which they make their living."

"And that is?"

"Divination," Mevreš said. "To the common people it's mere fortune-telling—and I will admit to you, if not publicly, that in many cases it's a sham. There is more money, and more safety, to be had in telling people what they want to hear. But the art itself is real enough. The Korenat use it among themselves for the good of their people; each caravan is expected to have its own diviners, husband and wife. I came to this group because they had lost theirs, and needed someone to train replacements."

The Korenat did a lot of things in husband-and-wife couples. One of the stories Mevreš had told her on the road was about the creation of human beings; the Korenat said they had been made in pairs, male and female. "If you can do this kind of thing, why didn't you use it to get out of the mountains on your own?"

He smiled ruefully. "Our lives would be a good deal easier if it worked in that straightforward a fashion. No, I'm afraid it can't be used to draw a map to our destination—though had we not encountered you, I would have done my best to guide us, by any means available to me."

Ree hooked the toe of one boot over the other foot.

"So this can't find the rebels, either."

"Not directly, no. But I do think it could be of use."

"How?"

"Ask me a question," Mevreš said. "We will sit down somewhere, out of view, and I will count the days for you, and tell you what I hear."

What did I give up to the Lhian? The question tried so hard to leap out of her mouth, Ree had to clench her jaw to keep it inside. There was no way in any hell she would ask Mevreš that. Not even if he could answer it for her. Maybe especially if he could.

It would have to be something where she had a reasonable chance of judging his accuracy, without being a subject he might have learned about by other means. After all, he'd already admitted that sometimes this was a sham.

"All right," she said, and shoved herself off the wall. "Follow me."

• • •

They went out of the city, to the spindly shade of a tree near the southern road. For comfort it was less than ideal, but anywhere in Taraspai carried too high a risk of them being interrupted . . . or overheard. And the question Ree had decided to ask wasn't one she wanted anybody hearing, not even Aadet.

The grass hadn't yet burned brown in the summer's heat, but it was well on its way. Ree sat cross-legged in a thick patch of it; Mevreš sat facing her, but with the soles of his feet together and his back very straight.

I've done this before, she thought, seeing his posture. Not with him, but other Korenat in other lifetimes. A woman—she could see the face, though she couldn't remember the name. Older. *What did I ask her?* The memory was frustratingly incomplete. She knew Mevreš was sitting that way because he shouldn't cross any part of his body while performing the ritual, but she couldn't remember who had taught her that.

He reached inside his shirt and drew out a bundle shaped like the leaf-wrapped dumplings the Korenat ate at every meal. This one was made of fabric, though, and bound with a leather thong. Holding it between his hands, he spoke for a time in a low, rapid voice—Korenat words.

Ree kept her expression blank. Five days among the Nevati; five days unmasked. It was enough for her to make good progress with their language. On a first hearing, a strange tongue was as unfamiliar to her as to anybody else, but the process of learning was a thousandfold faster. If she heard words translated, or spoken in a context where she could guess at their meaning, she never forgot them. It didn't take much before she started picking up grammar, and from there it was a cascade. Not memory—though no doubt she'd learned plenty of these languages in past lives, or older forms of them. It was just a gift, her nature as an archon.

She understood part of what Mevreš was saying, and picked up more as he went along. He was praying, invoking Korenat spirits and features in the landscape. Not the landscape of Solaike; she didn't know what place he was describing. But she did catch him posing the question she'd given him: "What are Kaistun's feelings toward this woman?"

She wondered whether Mevreš thought the question was a romantic one. When people went to diviners, that was often what they worried about: *Does he love me? Should I marry him?* Romance was the furthest thing from her mind. Survival . . . that was a good deal closer.

When his prayers were done, Mevreš untied the cord and unfolded the fabric to reveal a pile of seeds, with a small number of crystals mixed in. Good manners—and a little bit of caution—kept Ree from picking up one of the seeds, but she studied them curiously. "What are those? I've never seen anything like them before. Not that I'm an expert on seeds, of course."

"Çayem," Mevreš said. "It's a tree that grows in Krvos, the ancestral homeland. They're the traditional material for these bundles, but—well. Most Korenat daykeepers have to make do with something else."

Then I bet that's one of your icons. Archai came out of the apeiron with nothing, but over the course of a given lifetime they collected a scattering of objects that identified them from one existence to the next—assuming they survived long enough to collect anything. Ree had gotten hers fast, on the island of the Lhian, where the long residence of a free archon bent the ordinary rules of the world to suit its mistress' nature. She still didn't know what they meant: the red sash at her waist, the sabre at her hip, and the cool ember she wore beneath her shirt.

Thinking of icons made her frown. "You aren't going to unmask?"

"What I'm doing here isn't an archon gift. Humans learn to count the days, too."

"Will it go better if you do?"

He paused, which told her the answer even before he replied. "It might."

"Then unmask. I'll let you know if anybody's approaching close enough to tell."

Mevreš didn't hesitate, which also told her something. *He trusts me to watch his back..*

He laid out the fabric, which was embroidered with intricate, colorful patterns that closely echoed the strip of fabric draping his shoulders. With his right hand he mixed the seeds and crystals, repeating phrases from his opening prayer. Then he plucked out the crystals, laying them out one by one in an arrangement that meant nothing to Ree, invoking each with a brief call. Once these were separated out, he mixed the seeds once more, blew into his hand, and grabbed a handful from the pile, pushing the rest to the side.

Ree watched with interest as he began to sort the seeds into piles of four, laying them in tidy rows. "Can I ask questions?" she said. "Or will that distract you?" Then she snorted. "Two questions right there. Feel free to tell me to shut up."

Mevreš smiled up at her. "It won't distract me, not right now. But please don't interrupt when I begin chanting."

"Fair enough. Can you tell me what you're doing?"

His smile became a laugh. "For me to answer that completely would take two hundred and sixty days."

"That's an oddly specific number."

"It's the number of days in the ritual calendar. Initiating a daykeeper requires one full cycle, and a complete explanation would mean initiating you. But to give you a briefer answer: I'm going to be calling on the Day Lords, the spirits of the ritual calendar, to hear your question and respond. They will answer me as I count the days; which day they answer on will tell me something about the question you asked. It may take multiple arrangements of the seeds to address the whole question. Some things are answered clearly and quickly, while others require more effort."

He was watching her as he said all of this, the same way he'd watched her while he told stories on the trip down to Taraspai. *Waiting for me to suddenly remember that I'm Korenat.* She shoved the thought aside and said, "Go ahead."

Mevreš began to chant. She picked out the numbers immediately, cycling from one to thirteen and then repeating. The other words came through more sporadically. She heard some she recognized, like "deer" and "bird" and "dawn," but others were unfamiliar. After a time, though, she realized they were repeating just like the numbers did. Thirteen numbers; twenty names; they cycled at different rates, with One Bird coming back around the next time as Eight Bird, and then as Two Bird. Two hundred and sixty days in the ritual calendar—the point at which both cycles would return to their start at the same time. Mevreš's explanation made more sense now.

He wasn't just counting, though. Here and there he paused, always at the end of his layout of little piles, but sometimes also in the middle. Whenever he did so, he spoke, and the fact that he spoke mostly in trade tongue didn't make his words much more comprehensible to her. "*Vlaya,*" he said at the end of his first pass. It was the

Korenat word for "deer"; then he shifted languages. "He has mounted his obstacles. A strong man—but Vlaya's strength can be for both good and ill." He resumed his count, but only made it five piles into the second pass before he stopped again. "Çe. The good road, the straight road, the long road. Not an evil man, then, but a good one, a leader."

Ree clamped her hands in her lap to avoid fidgeting. The longer she sat there, the more her body began to tingle, as if there were lightning in her veins. It was a thing that happened to her sometimes, but never like this. It usually coincided with blood: a sacrificed bull, a cauldron full of crimson. Mevreš was just counting. But her own blood had sparked in reply the first time she saw him, and now it was as if her body was responding to those two conflicting rhythms, thirteen numbers, twenty names, until she would have given her teeth just to make them harmonize.

Mevreš didn't seem to notice. And between the distracting sensations and his unpredictable words, Ree got comprehensively lost. If this was a sham, he was a master of obfuscation, throwing out so many seeming non sequiturs that she went cross-eyed trying to see how they were connected. She just gave up and waited for him to be done.

When he finally finished, he scooped the seeds and

crystals back together and laid his hands over them. "Thanks be to the homeland earth," he said in the Korenat tongue, then took up one last handful, kissed it, and tied the bundle back together.

The sensation of lightning faded, much to Ree's relief. "Okay," she said. "What the hell did that mean?"

"Each of the Day Lords has associations," Mevreš said. "If they speak—"

"I don't care how it works. You could make up complete nonsense for an explanation and I wouldn't know any better. What answer do you have for my question?"

Mevreš put the bundle away, mouth set in a pensive line. After a moment, the red of his veins faded back into the warm brown of his skin. "He is grateful to you, this Kaistun. You saved him once, didn't you? Saved his life, or something else of equal value—he owes you a great debt, and he knows it. But at the same time, he fears you."

"I have no intention of threatening him."

"No intention, perhaps—but you are an archon. Your very presence in Solaike might be a problem for him. He breathes a sigh of relief whenever you're gone, and each time, a part of him hopes you will never come back. And he is ashamed of this impulse." Mevreš paused, clearly wrestling with himself. Then he said, "What is his real name? No one calls him Kaistun, I'm sure of it."

"Enkettsivaane," Ree said. "And you should probably

get in the habit of saying that instead, because using the king's personal name after he takes the staff is punishable by death."

Mevreš's whole body jerked.

"Sorry," Ree said. She meant it: annoyance at Mevreš wasn't reason enough to lure him into a capital crime. "But I needed to be sure you weren't getting your information from some other source, and using this whole show as a cover."

He pinched the bridge of his nose, eyes crinkling shut. "You're a very suspicious woman, you know that?"

"It's in my nature." Ree leaned back and stretched her legs out, angling her body so she wouldn't kick Mevreš. Her fingers dug into the thick grass. "I'm not surprised I make him nervous. I make a lot of people nervous, here especially. They've been arguing about it since he took the staff, what they should do about archai. The stories say that the kings of Solaike used to be attended by their own ancestors—the archai who supposedly founded their lineages. Some people insist Enkettsivaane has to call up his own ancestral archon, to legitimize his lineage holding the staff."

"Unless his summoners are exceedingly skilled," Mevreš said, "they would end up with dozens of stray archai wandering the kingdom before they got the right one."

"Not if they banished them all. And by 'banish,' of course I mean 'kill.'" Mevreš looked sick, but Ree went on without giving him a chance to find his tongue. "Valtaja wasn't from one of the old noble families. He had no ancestral archon, and he didn't like the idea of anything destabilizing his control, so he had all the skilled summoners killed, along with the bound archon who served the previous king. Summoning an archon was made a capital crime. Some people think Enkettsivaane should have maintained that ban—and he might put it back. But it's a little awkward for him to welcome me at court while saying that nobody like me should ever be called into Solaike again."

"Or like me." Mevreš brooded, linking his fingers together. "So you think I should not reveal myself. Even if I could help."

"I didn't say that." Ree tipped her head back, looking at the sky through the scraggled branches of the tree. There were a dozen reasons why she couldn't stay in Solaike, from her inability to sleep more than three nights in the same bed to the king's justifiable fear that her presence would warp the world around her, remaking it in her own image. That was what happened when archai lived for long enough in one place. It was how the Lhian's island had been created.

But even if the king welcomed her, even if she moved

to a new room every three days, she still couldn't make this place her home. Because that was the one thing she could not have.

So she came and went, leaving because she had to, and returning because Aadet was here. He was the first friend she'd made in this life, and this was *his* home. So she kept coming back—and the knife twisted a little deeper every time she did.

Her own situation wasn't the problem right now. Mevreš's was. She said, "You can't stay here, not in the long run. I know you weren't planning to anyway, but we'll need to make it clear to them that you're not going to try."

Mevreš sat up straighter. "So you think I *should* offer my help."

Ree smiled sourly. "I don't know what your Day Lords say about our future, but I have a bad feeling we'll need all the help we can get."

• • •

They faced the king in full court, kneeling like petitioners in front of the latticed fence that divided the royal dais from the rest of the courtyard. Mevreš didn't hesitate to show all the deference Solaine protocol demanded: an artifact of his people's travels, maybe, which made deference necessary to survival. Ree wasn't sure how long the Korenat had been wanderers—whether they'd begun their journey before or after the gods and higher powers exiled the archai to the apeiron and forbade any more to be made.

Questions like that would have to wait. Mevreš was masked; Ree wasn't, and her black clothing stood out like an ink blot among the brighter colors of the king's court. The sun beat down on her without mercy, while Enkettsivaane and all his ministers enjoyed the shade. She knelt a pace ahead of Mevreš, almost at the fence itself, and bowed low. "Father of the Nation, you have shown me great kindness in permitting me to reside not only in your kingdom, not only in your capital city, but within the walls of your very palace."

Everyone in the courtyard could hear her perfectly well, but one of the king's wives inclined her head, turned, and bent to repeat her words into the king's ear. Ree had been at court sessions a few times, and she found the practice of carrying on the whole conversation through an intermediary to be incredibly tedious . . . but now that she was a petitioner on the other side of the lattice, she also had to admit it had an effect. *You aren't important enough for the king to hear you directly.* On her, the effect was mostly annoying, because she'd known Enkettsivaane when he was covered in mud and didn't have two coins to rub together. But for the people he needed to impress, she suspected it worked.

I wonder if one of his predecessors was hard of hearing, and that's how this whole process got started?

Entertaining as the thought was, Ree knew she was trying to distract herself. Mevreš had said it, after his divination: the king was both grateful to and afraid of her. Today's business might tip him toward the latter half of that balance. She could end this afternoon with the news that she was no longer welcome in Solaike at all.

Ree waited when the king's wife was done, but he had no reply for her. Not yet.

So she went on. "The Sixfold Blessed One has demonstrated his great prudence in the matter of the usurper's ban against my kind. To maintain it would be to deprive the Solaine people of their heritage, and of powers that might work to their benefit. But to welcome every passing archon would be . . . reckless." She almost said "stupid." Speaking at court always made her tongue clumsy; she wanted to speak plainly, but the fashion here was to embroider every sentence.

Once this had been repeated for the king's benefit, Ree gestured to Mevreš, kneeling a pace behind. "Strong Hand Upon the Staff, if I have been of use to you in the past"—*which we both know I have*—"then I ask you to consider my words today, when I recommend this man to your attention. He is an archon of the Korenat, a wise elder to their people. It was his intention to leave the Nevati caravan here and move onward to another group of Korenat who might benefit from his guidance. But hearing of the insolence of Sihpo Teglane and his so-called Red Leopard, he has offered to remain for a short while longer and give what assistance he can to the expedition led by your honored wife Aadet Temini."

None of this was a surprise to the king or his ministers, of course. Springing an archon on him in public, without warning, would have been sheer idiocy. Ree had talked to Aadet, who had talked to a senior wife, who had talked to a minister, who had talked to the king. It was a longer and more annoying chain of communication than the one she faced now. But it meant she didn't have to wait now for the king to consider what his response would be, because he'd already decided.

Springing his decision on *her* as a surprise: that was fair game.

Ree held her breath.

And then let it out again a moment later, because no matter what the king did today, it wouldn't happen that fast. But she took it as an encouraging sign when he called for Mevreš to approach the fence—surely he wouldn't bother with that if he was going to throw one or both archai out? Speaking through his intermediary,

Enkettsivaane questioned Mevreš, finding out how long he'd been in the world (he answered honestly, or at least with the same answer he'd given Ree), how long he'd been with this particular Nevati caravan, and more.

Then Mevreš said, "Father of the Nation. May I have your leave to answer a question you have not asked?"

Murmurs answered him from around the courtyard. Mevreš's words came perilously close to implying the king was a fool, failing to ask something obvious. But the king, after some consideration, said, "Speak."

Mevreš bowed. "Exalted of the Many, any given archon often lives and dies without having enough time to recall their true nature in full. I have been blessed with many years in this lifetime—enough years to know myself. You have not asked me to explain my nature, but with your permission, I will do so now. And I will unmask, so you may see me for what I am."

Ree found she was holding her breath again. Volunteering that information like this, in public . . . was he stupidly brave? Or just confident that nobody here would—or could—harm him?

The king's wives murmured amongst themselves. Ree could guess well enough what was coming. Guards pushed their way through the audience to ring the two of them where they knelt in the courtyard, took up new stations, and aimed their guns at the two archai. *Great. If they decide to take him out, I'm going down with him.*

"Careful," she muttered through her teeth.

He didn't acknowledge her, or the guards. He merely waited until the king's intermediary said, "Continue."

Mevreš bowed in thanks and unmasked, displaying his glimmering red veins for the world to see. The smoke of his breath pluming the air, he said, "The truth of my nature may be seen in my skin. I might best be described as the bonds which hold the Korenat together as a people, although they have been scattered across the world, and now travel under a dozen different names. I am their kinship: the blood ties that bind them together.

"Blood is the fundamental fact of the Korenat world. Our myths say the sun did not move in the sky, the earth did not bear fruit, until it was gifted with blood. That is the means by which we speak to the spirits and the gods, the coin in which our heavens trade. All other valuable things we sacrifice or trade in—gold, gems, the beautiful craftsmanship of our hands—are metaphors for this most precious coin, so that our word for 'debt' is a close cousin to our word for 'blood.' And so, when we speak of owing someone a debt, we speak of owing them blood.

"I mean no harm to your people or your land, and I think it is unlikely that I will inflict it on them. My presence brings wholeness for the Korenat, a renewal of their kinship with each other and their more distant cousins."

Mevreš bowed again, this time placing his hands on his knees in a style unlike the bows of Solaike. "But your hospitality to this Nevati caravan would place us in your debt. On behalf of my people, I wish to pay that debt—even if it means risking my own life in the mountains against your foes. Thus do I offer you the blood we owe."

Silence fell. Ree's fingers ached from digging into the unyielding flagstones of the courtyard. The lightning was back, in her veins, in her blood. *Blood is the fundamental fact of the Korenat world.*

But if that were true, why could she not remember them?

It gaped within her like an open wound, that lack. She screamed inside her own mind, a demand that her spirit regain some tiny fragment of itself, a memory or another syllable of her true name, *anything* that would confirm Mevreš's claim that she was Korenat. Or prove him wrong—she would be happy either way. Anything would be preferable to this echoing silence in her head.

Nothing came. Ree missed what the others said next, the wife's repetition of Mevreš's words and the king's reply. She only came back to her senses when the king stood: a sign that he was about to make a formal proclamation.

For this, he spoke in his own voice, directly to his

people and his petitioners. It was a voice Ree had heard hundreds of times before, whispering a warning through the trees or bellowing commands across a battlefield. It would never be called resonant, but it carried the self-assurance of a man who did not question—or let others question—the certainty that his words would be obeyed.

"We have given much thought to the question of archai in our kingdom. This is our decision: that they neither be banned, nor given free rein. To summon an archon without royal approval is henceforth punishable by death . . . but those lineages who wish to study the art may petition for our approval. To bring a bound archon within our borders without declaring its presence to our guards and soldiers is likewise a crime, to be punished by exile or death as we see fit. To be a free archon within our borders without declaring one's nature will bring exile or death."

His gaze fell to the two kneeling before him. "To those free archai we permit to enter the kingdom, license will be granted to remain for no longer than a period of one month. After departing, they may not return until a full year has passed. By these means do we grant to our people the benefits of their kind, and protect our land against the influence of those whose nature bends the world around them."

Ree's breath came fast. *One month. One year.* It wasn't much different from her usual behavior—just formalized. She had no doubt the king had calculated with that in mind. The debt he owed her was not forgotten, but she didn't have free rein, either. *No more coming in unannounced.*

She could live with it. But depending on whether he meant to count from today or the day she'd crossed the border, she didn't have long to help Aadet . . . and neither did Mevreš.

This wasn't the time to ask. Along with Mevreš, Ree bowed low, while all around them the court shouted the ritualized phrases, to mark that they heard and heeded their sovereign's words.

• • •

"Of course you still have a month," Aadet said. "If he didn't want to give you that time, he would have waited to make his decree until your time was nearly up."

"Well, shit," Ree said with a grin. "I guess I can't use that as my excuse to skip out on the hard work, then."

There was no point calculating the balance of debt between the two of them. It had long since passed any possibility of repayment; they helped each other how and when they could. And this felt right, striding out of Taraspai side by side, the mountains rising up ahead like a green wall. They'd been happy there, both of them, and they were happy to return—even with the trouble waiting for them, in the form of the Red Leopard.

Decree or no decree, the soldiers were uncertain what to do with the archon in their midst. Not Ree; Aadet had picked veterans, people who remembered her from the days of the revolution. With her, they fell back into the familiar habits of the past. But they didn't know Mevreš, apart from rumors about the Korenat and what they'd heard about his speech in court.

Ree hadn't said anything to him yet about that speech. She was still trying to figure out what it meant for her. Until that question got answered, she was happy to keep herself busy with Solaike's problems.

Mevreš took the soldiers' suspicions in stride, and neither forced his company on them, nor held himself so far aloof that he would seem even more alien than he already did. He told stories—first to Ree and Aadet, then to groups when they stopped for the night—and as the days went by this got him a measure of goodwill from the soldiers. They'd all been fugitives in the mountains, where the only forms of entertainment available to them were the ones that needed nothing more than a body and a voice.

Seimer, Ree thought. She was sure of it now. If he embodied the blood ties that bound the Korenat together, then he had to be ruled by his *seimer* aspect; there was nothing of destruction in that, not even the good kind. But he had a *gemer* aspect, too—every archon did. What was his? Their exile and scattering across the world? Or maybe the Korenat fought each other sometimes, internecine feuds made worse by their common kinship. She didn't know enough about them to guess.

The journey began easily enough, along the main trade road, with no attempt to travel in secret. In fact, Aadet had deliberately let word of his plans slip, knowing it would be picked up by the rebels' eyes and ears in the city. Keeping the entire thing under wraps would have been impossible, and one of the most trusted ministers had agents watching the most likely spies; they'd tracked a handful of people leaving Taraspai who might be going to warn the rebels. The warning hardly mattered—Sihpo Teglane's force couldn't get much harder to find than they were already—but the path the informants took once they neared the mountains might give Aadet some notion of where to start his search.

Two days' journey from the city, their force split up and began traveling cross-country in smaller groups, to hide their precise location and movements from any rebel watchers. They regrouped in the foothills, and there Aadet laid out the pattern of their search.

He didn't use a map. When the revolutionaries were

the ones hiding in the mountains, maps had been a liability; all it took was a single one falling into enemy hands, and half their refuges would be compromised. Instead he described routes and search areas in terms of landmarks, their usual way of navigating. Their total force he split into four parts, to cover more ground, and arranged for scouts to run the circuit between each group so they could stay informed of each others' movements.

It was a good plan—and it got them absolutely nowhere.

They tramped up and down any number of valleys, looking for the Red Leopard. It was almost like the old days, moving in stealth beneath the high branches, signaling by hand when the enemy might be close. Ree's body and mind fell easily into the rhythm of it. But instead of retreating to cover, they were hunting through it, looking in every concealed rock shelter, every ravine that seemed completely choked with vegetation, but if you got under the canopy of it you found there was enough room to move.

Oh, they found the signs they were looking for. Cold firepits, trampled greenery, the butchered bones of forest antelope and other game animals. But all of it was days old, nothing recent, nothing they could use as a lead. And some of the encampments had been made in places they shouldn't have known about, little dells and caverns that had stayed unknown to Valtaja's men when it was

Kaistun's followers hiding out here.

The third time that happened, Aadet kicked a charred branch-end into the wall of the rock shelter. "Damn it. How long have they been out here? You can stumble onto a place like this, but again and again? They haven't had enough time to find so many."

"Maybe it isn't time they've got," Ree said. "Maybe they have something else."

He stared at her. "No. None of our people would—"

"Are you sure? Do you know where every former revolutionary is? Can you swear none of them would take a fat bribe, or the promise of founding their own lineage when Sihpo comes to power?"

It echoed what he'd said back in Taraspai, about somebody there funding the rebels. But neither of them had extended their suspicions this far, all the way to the men and women who had stayed by Kaistun's side during the long years of their forest war.

We should have thought of it before now.

Aadet stared blindly at the stone wall. "I hate this," he breathed, shoulders rising with tension. "The politics of it. I thought—after I went to the Lhian—"

He'd traded blood for the inspiration necessary to make his people believe a revolution could succeed. At the time, that had seemed like the biggest obstacle in the world to him. Nothing else would have mattered if he couldn't clear that hurdle . . . but now he was on the far side of it, and the path there was even more treacherous than the one before.

"We'll figure it out," Ree said. The rest of the soldiers had already left the shelter; there was no one to see her transgressing royal law. She reached out and gripped Aadet's shoulder, digging in hard enough to bring him back to himself. *They can flog me for touching the king's wife later.* "If there's a traitor—and we don't know for sure that there is—it doesn't make the Red Leopard invincible. It just makes this a little more annoying, is all."

She felt the tremor as he let out his breath. "Annoying. Is that what you call it."

"I could use other words, but they'd be less polite."

The tremor became a ghost of a laugh. Then Aadet inhaled deeply, and she let go of his shoulder. "All right," he said. "First, let's find out if we're just imagining things."

Mevreš was sitting on the trunk of a fallen tree outside, but he shot to his feet when Aadet came sweeping out of the cave. "Yes, honored royal wife?"

"That thing of yours." Aadet gestured, a sharp flail of his hand that betrayed the frustration and impatience not far beneath the surface. "Get it out. Tell me if we have a traitor on our hands, and that's why we can't find these bastards."

"It'll take a little while," Mevreš said. "And I'll need a

flat surface." The area around him was mazed with ferns and underbrush, thriving where the fallen tree had allowed sunlight through to the ground.

They ended up using the tree itself, planing down its trunk with machetes until it approximated a table just large enough for Mevreš's cloth. Every soldier in their squadron would have crowded around to watch the archon do his work, if Ree hadn't driven them off with sharp words and sharper elbows. "Get your asses out of here. Keep an eye on our surroundings—you want those bastards ambushing us while he's staring at his seeds?" They listened, mostly, and left the three of them in relative peace.

A single arrangement was enough to give Mevreš his answer. "*Zhuyin*," he said, and the fact that his handful of seeds came out in even piles of four meant the answer was certain. Someone from the revolutionaries had gone over to Sihpo Teglane's side, teaching the rebels how to hide in the mountains, using the same tricks that had kept Enkettsivaane's followers safe for so long.

Aadet didn't bother to hide his fury. He stormed off before Mevreš was even done binding up his divination bundle. Ree followed; judging by the looks on the faces of his soldiers, she was the only one who dared do it anymore. They knew him from the old days, but he was the king's wife now. No longer a simple soldier.

Some old habits died hard; others didn't die at all. Aadet kept going until he found a sheltered spot, overhung by vines, just large enough for him to sit cross-legged and Ree to crouch nearby. The uneven footing strained her ankles, but she waited without complaint until Aadet was done swearing, in a low, vicious tone that didn't carry past the vines.

When his most recent pause grew long enough to sound more like a halt, she said, "What now?" Then she shook her head. "Stupid question. We keep going, of course."

"What else can we do?" Aadet said, jaw setting in an uncompromising line. "The king is hunting for traitors at home; if the gods are generous, he'll find them, and then the Red Leopard will at least lose their support. But we'll still have to dig them out of the mountains."

"You could try to set bait. Fill a caravan with soldiers, send it along the main road, and see if they bite."

"That would get us some of them, but not all. Not enough." He braced his elbows on his knees and brooded. "We need Sihpo Teglane. Him and all of his lieutenants. And if he's smart, he won't commit himself personally to an attack. Assuming we can even send a bait caravan without him knowing it's a trap, which is probably optimistic."

Ree shifted position, trying to find a more comfortable way to crouch. "Then layer the traps three deep.

Send a bait caravan, make him think that's you trying to distract him from something else important—a shipment of coin or weapons or whatever—fill those wagons with explosives or something—"

Aadet buried his hands in his hair. "You never give up, do you?" Then he snorted. "Of course not. It's in your nature."

He was half right. Ree didn't know her own story, not the way Mevreš knew his, but the instinct to pit herself against everything in her path was carved into her bones. It was the same impulse that had sent her over that deer track in the mountains, just to see if she could make it.

But that was only half of her nature.

"For now," she said. "Speaking of which."

His head came up sharply. He'd forgotten again—because he had the luxury of forgetting. "Ree," Aadet said, "you don't have to go."

"Yes, I do. You don't want me around here during the new moon. And to be honest—" The downside to being shielded from view was, it made it harder to tell if anybody was eavesdropping. Ree went on, more quietly. "I'd rather not show Mevreš this side of me just yet."

"You don't trust him?"

She snorted. "You know me. The list of people I do trust is pretty damn short."

"Yes, I know you," Aadet said, his voice steady. "And I

know when you're brushing me off."

Ree shifted again. Her ankles were beginning to seriously ache. *Aadet could have picked a better place to hole up and brood.* "Look, he's an archon. That right there is enough to make me twitchy. But he—" The words stuck in her throat. Finally she said, "He thinks he knows something about what I am, but I'm not so sure. It ought to ring true, and it doesn't. Until I sort that out, I don't want to give him any more ammunition."

Aadet knew when not to argue. His hand on her shoulder was a comforting weight—a reminder that however much had changed between them, this hadn't. Even if they could only touch when no one else was around to see.

And better he do it now than tomorrow.

"Then do what you have to," Aadet said. "We'll see you in three days."

• • •

It always woke her up.

Ree couldn't see the moon from her perch in the crook of a tree, but she didn't have to. She knew the moment it broke the horizon, a crescent too thin and pale to see in the grey light of dawn. Like a magnet to iron, the new moon called to her soul—and the *gemer* half answered.

Weight settled on her like lead. Dawn's light didn't bring the bright possibility of a new day; it was thin and damp with the forest's oppressive humidity, and what the fuck did she think she was going to accomplish out here, anyway?

Nothing. She'd known that before she left Aadet's squadron, even though she was in her *seimer* aspect then.

Seimer and *gemer,* the two faces that made up her coin. Every archon's coin, no matter where they hailed from or how long they'd been in the world. Creation on one side; destruction on the other. However those impulses manifested in any given case.

For Ree, it was about hope. Most days she was ruled by her *seimer* half, and believed that whatever trials she faced, she would find a way to overcome them. To survive whatever the world threw at her. To win through. But for the three days of the new moon, her *gemer* aspect took control . . . and then she saw things very differently.

It was always tempting, outside the new moon, to see this as an aberration. A temporary depression, a fleeting bit of pessimism she would shake off in due course. But Ree knew better. Her *gemer* half was as true as its counterpart, its fatalistic predictions as plausible as their hopeful cousins. She could tell herself as much as she liked that finding the rebels was just a matter of searching hard enough, but the truth was that Aadet's revolutionaries had hidden in these mountains for a generation, and the soldiers had never dug them out. If the rebels had a turncoat advising them, then it might be a generation more before they could be captured and destroyed. Assuming Sihpo Teglane didn't cripple trade into Solaike thoroughly enough to topple the king and start the civil war all over again.

Her *seimer* half might not want to think about that possibility, but hiding from it didn't change a thing.

She leaned her head back against the trunk of the tree and sighed. This was the darkness the Lhian had lifted from her, years ago—but that deal hadn't taken it away, not entirely. Whatever the other archon had claimed as her price, it put Ree into her *seimer* aspect; at the time, Ree had expected that change to last. The first new moon after leaving the island had broken her of that notion. No archon expressed only one half of their nature: even someone like Mevreš, who seemed to be as *seimer* as they got, had his destructive side.

Unless he's playing us all, building up our trust so he can betray us later.

No. Even right now, when she saw the dark alternatives so much more clearly, she didn't believe that.

But she had hoped—foolishly—that the new moon might bring her some much-needed clarity. Aadet's deal with the Lhian had been blood for inspiration: his blood, her inspiration. Ree's deal had gone the other way. She took blood, and in return, the Lhian took . . . something. Ree had never been able to figure out what, even though its effects were unmistakable. Then along came Mevreš, telling her she was Korenat. Words that rang hollow and false.

She'd started to wonder if that was what the Lhian took from her—the part of her story that connected her to Zhutore's long-dead ancestors. After all, blood was the fundamental fact of the Korenat world, and Ree had paid for blood.

But the logic of it didn't quite work. If the Lhian had taken that connection, how could Mevreš recognize her as Korenat? And it didn't explain the new moon, these three days where the weight of it all came crashing back—but Ree had half-wondered if she *would* remember, once the moon rose. If the Lhian's deal only held force twenty-five days out of the month, then maybe on the other three, Ree would know herself for what she was.

So much for that hope. She looked inside, and found nothing.

It could still be true, both parts of it. She might be Korenat, and that connection, or at least the awareness of it, might be what the Lhian had taken from her. But it didn't matter either way. She was still out here in the forest, by herself, and the odds of her accomplishing a damned thing were vanishingly small.

All the same, it was better than the alternative. She'd left as much to get away from Aadet's people as from Mevreš. For these three days, she was a danger to everyone around her, because a single touch was enough to infect them with the fatalism of her *gemer* aspect. Not to mention that people rarely wanted to hear what she had to say, her honest evaluation of their situation and their chances. There were a few instances where her contagious darkness was of use to the revolutionaries—one battle in particular, when she managed to get at the enemy commander the night before and poison his hopes of success until he made a series of idiotic mistakes the following day—but on the whole, she was better off alone.

Yet another reason she could never stay in Solaike, regardless of the law.

Even in her *gemer* aspect, though, Ree wasn't much inclined to cool her heels in a tree until the moon changed. She swung down, her muscles protesting the long hours of carefully balanced stillness. She might as well move.

Part of her sometimes thought she should spend her whole life like this, traveling the wilderness, where it didn't much matter whether she was *seimer* or *gemer*. She always felt right when she was in motion; she could lose herself in the trance of it, her legs working tirelessly while the small part of her mind that remained alert considered which path to take. And for someone who couldn't spend more than three nights in the same bed, it made sense. Sure, there was always the risk that she might be eaten by a leopard or other local predator—but the human world had its own dangers, equally lethal, and often less honest.

But she knew it would never work. Wandering was only part of her nature; she also needed words. Conversation, stories, interaction. She would go mad if she had nobody to talk to, as mad as she would if somebody chained her to one spot.

Three days wasn't a problem, though. She could do three days of silence just fine.

Her feet took her up and down the valleys, along ridges and into the hidden folds of the forest, searching because there was no reason not to. Here and there she found signs of a human presence, but never anything substantial enough to make her think it was the rebels. More likely hunters, or lone outlaws hiding from the king's judgment. Ree didn't much care what crimes the latter had committed, unless her appearance panicked them into attacking. *And if they do? They'll deserve what they get.*

She didn't pay very much attention to where she was going. At any point she could climb a ridge or a tree and spot enough landmarks to have a general sense of her location; until she found something useful, the specifics didn't matter. She just walked, and waited for the new moon to end, and knew that nothing would be different when it did.

At twilight on the final day she stopped to rinse her face in a stream, washing away a layer of sweat and grime. The coolness of the water was pleasant enough that she cupped some of it into her hand and drank, even though she didn't need to. Then she sat back on her heels and closed her eyes, sighing.

Three days wasted. A good match for the wasted weeks that had preceded them. But she would never talk Aadet into giving up, and *seimer* or *gemer*, she would never try.

Lightning danced in her blood, and she opened her eyes.

She almost didn't see it, in the deepening shadows beneath the trees. If the cat hadn't blinked, she might never have spotted it. But it did, and she did, and only instinct kept Ree from reaching for her blade—an instinct that said if she tried, the beast would be on her before the weapon cleared its sheath.

At first she thought it was a leopard. Black ones were rare, but not unheard of; there were several pelts in the king's palace, prized for their unusual color. The cat was certainly big enough to be a leopard. *Too* big, in fact. Its head was heavy, its bent legs stocky and powerful; at full stretch, Ree thought it would stand a foot taller at the shoulder than a leopard.

In the end, though, it didn't really matter what kind of cat it was. Because no normal cat of any kind had eyes that gleamed blood-red in the fading light.

It crouched on the far side of the stream, one good bound away. Ree stayed where she was, not even moving a finger, hardly daring to breathe. What the fuck else could she do? She was alone in the forest, like a god-damned idiot; nobody could come to her rescue. Even if she'd drawn her sabre, she didn't really want to bet on it against a predator that weighed four hundred pounds. She had one weapon; it had five, and that was assuming she counted its four paws instead of each razor-sharp claw on them.

Though if it came to that, she would fight. The cat would take her out, but she'd make it bleed for its victory.

The cat didn't move. Neither did she. Around them both, the light continued to fade. *Are we going to sit here all night?*

In one smooth shift, the cat rose to its feet. Without a sound, it turned and began walking into the night. And Ree, without thinking, followed.

What the ever-loving fuck am I doing?

She had no rational explanation for it, and not much

of an irrational one, either. Just the way the cat's blood-colored eyes had lingered on her as it cast one final glance over its shoulder, and the way her own blood had sparked in response. Which didn't justify walking after a four-hundred-pound predator, just because it had red eyes and made the lightning dance—but here she was, doing it anyway.

The creature couldn't be an archon. They were all basically human in shape, allowing for a certain amount of variety. Could any of them shape-shift? Maybe; Ree's memories were nowhere near extensive enough to tell her. But there was no damned reason a strange archon would show up out of nowhere and then walk away, expecting Ree to follow.

No, not expecting. But giving her the chance.

For one wild moment, she wondered if the cat was actually Mevreš in a different form. His veins glowed red; so did the cat's eyes. And he, at least, had a reason to help her. But nothing about him had seemed feline, and besides, the cat was female. Ree had a vague recollection of once encountering an archon whose *seimer* and *gemer* aspects were male and female, but changing both sex *and* shape seemed like a bit much. And Mevreš, she thought, wouldn't have just walked away like that.

Wherever the cat was taking her, she hoped it wasn't far. The light was vanishing at speed; pretty soon Ree wouldn't be able to see where she put her feet, much less a black cat in a black forest. Already she was having to strain her eyes, following the creature less by seeing her than by tracking where the darkness moved. Then Ree's feet began to catch against roots and drop unexpectedly into dips in the ground, and she knew that if she kept on going, she was going to break her ankle, and maybe some other bones, too.

She also knew that if she stopped, the cat would leave her without a second glance. And she doubted she would see it again.

So stop. There was no point risking her neck when she didn't even know what, if anything, she would get in return.

But why had the cat appeared to her in the first place? Why put her in motion, if not for a purpose?

Ree's stride faltered. Even in that instant of hesitation, she almost lost sight of her guide. And that, against all logic and reason, decided her.

Fuck it. Let's see what happens.

Ree followed the cat into the night.

. . .

She couldn't see a goddamned thing. Not the cat, not the trees, not her own hand in front of her face. It was a moonless night, the last of the new moon, and what little starlight came through the branches wasn't enough to do more than create patches of thinner blackness among the deeper ones. Ree didn't even know how she was still following the cat—couldn't even be sure she *was*, except that from time to time she would see a glimmer of red eyes. Unless she was hallucinating that, which was entirely possible.

But if so, her hallucinations were doing a remarkably good job of keeping her from falling off a cliff.

With no moon, no stars, and no sense of the landscape passing beneath her feet, there was no way to measure time. She might have left the world entirely; maybe she *had* fallen off a cliff, and now she was walking through the apeiron, the realm where archai waited in timeless nonexistence between death and a human calling them forth once more. Except that she doubted the apeiron had all the scents and sounds of a tropical forest, the owls hooting and the leaves rustling and the night flowers blooming.

One thing she didn't hear: the grunts and roars of the leopards she knew haunted this area. *I don't blame you all for staying away from this thing.*

On and on she walked, in blind faith, until she began to think she would walk forever.

But the darkness began to lighten. At first so imperceptibly, she assumed she was imagining it; then enough that she knew it was real. Dawn was coming. She hadn't died. And the cat—

The cat wasn't in front of her anymore. But a sheer drop-off was, and Ree grabbed hold of a tree just in time to keep herself from walking over the edge of it.

She bit down hard on the urge to swear. Like half the trees in this forest, the one she'd grabbed was well-defended by thorns, and one of them had stabbed deep into the heel of her hand. Ree drew it free and sucked at the wound, tasting the copper of her own blood.

What the hell just happened?

The last time she'd experienced anything like that night-long walk, it was on the Lhian's island. Could she have wandered into another archon's domain without knowing it? *Not a chance.* No archai had survived Valtaja's military coup, and even if one moved in after the revolution, it took time for their presence to shape the world around them. There was no way one could have been here long enough to do that, without the royal court at least catching a whisper of it.

Ree's mind, worrying at that question, left her eyes free to drift over the landscape below her.

Then she threw herself flat to the ground.

The encampment in the ravine below was well-concealed, but not perfectly. Wisps of smoke rose from cook-fires, not quite blending with the morning mist. Ree counted two fires, three—maybe four. Enough to indicate a sizable camp, more than any hunters or simple bandits would set up. And their concealment spoke of discipline, a commander with enough control to stop his men from just settling down wherever they felt comfortable.

She'd found the rebels. Or, more to the point, the cat had led her to them.

What she didn't know was *why*.

Maybe Sihpo Teglane had his own bound archon, of which the cat was an icon or something like that. *Can an animal be an icon?* She didn't know. Say it could: then obviously he'd sent the cat to lure her into a trap.

But if it was a trap, why hadn't it sprung?

Ree made a quick survey of the area, not moving from her spot. She recognized the notched peak of Ahvelu; she wasn't that far from where she'd come through into Solaike. Assuming she could retrace her steps to Aadet before the rebels had a chance to move on, he could bring his force in, trap them in this valley, and crush them with one blow.

A grin spread across her face. The moon was up, a pale sliver in the dawn; the three days were over. She was *seimer* again, and ready to get this done.

Knowing the rebels' location was only part of it, though. Ree edged back from the precipice, then worked her way around and down, trying to find a vantage point from which she could get at least a rough count of their numbers and equipment. The terrain didn't oblige her. *The only way I'm getting that count is if I walk into the middle of the camp and yell for them all to come out.* Ree had a healthy respect for her own skill with a blade, and turning *seimer* always made her a little giddy with self-confidence, but she wasn't stupid enough to push it that far.

She turned, and cursed under her breath. *Yeah. What was that about overconfidence?*

The commander of this group was smart and disciplined. Of course he would put out patrols—and one of them was approaching her position. They were pretty good, too, barely more than a ripple in the undergrowth of the forest. Ree had been hiding from eyes in the valley below, so she hadn't paid much attention to anything behind her; she was too exposed on that side, and trying to move to better cover would just draw their eyes to her.

Three of them, it looked like. Bad odds—unless she could take one of them out before they noticed her.

Ree focused on her clothing, masking as far as she could to make it blend with the forest around her. Her hair was dark enough not to stand out much, and her skin wasn't too pale. Her red sash was a different matter ... not to mention the gleaming blade of her sabre, but she had a knife in her boot, and she slipped that from its sheath, keeping it concealed behind her leg. Then she relaxed her muscles and waited for her moment.

The patrol's point man barely had time to look up before she slammed into him, sinking her knife into the side of his neck. He wasn't dead when they hit the ground, but he couldn't yell either, and at the moment that was all she cared about. Ree rolled and surged to her feet, sabre coming out; it slashed across the throat of the second man as he opened his mouth to shout. That left just one man whole, and those were odds she could deal with.

But he had a long gun, and he had time enough to raise it and fire.

Ree plowed into the dirt again. The bullet whined overhead, narrowly missing her. *Idiot.* She wasn't sure who she meant, herself or the gunman. She hadn't seen the weapon before she leapt—but he'd fired too quickly, not taking enough time to aim, and now he was left with a glorified club in his hands. Ree came up sabre-first, ripping open the inside of his thigh; he dropped a moment later.

Last woman standing—for all the good it does me. There was no way the encampment below hadn't heard that shot. She could escape before they found her, but the bodies would announce her presence anyway. And then the commander of this place would order his men to pull up stakes.

When she looked up from cleaning her blade, the cat was there again.

Ree locked eyes with the beast, black to red. The cat's lips skinned back, showing her teeth. And Ree, understanding, nodded.

The sounds began as she loped away through the forest: a wet ripping, the lap of the cat's tongue. They'd find three bodies, all right. Three corpses savaged by the predator they tried and failed to shoot. It might send them onward; it might not. Either way, Ree had to hurry.

She could think about the cat later.

• • •

Luckily Ree knew the direction Aadet intended to take his search during the new moon; otherwise she might have needed another feline visitation to find his new encampment. As it was, she got there just before sunset. His men had their guns up when she reached their perimeter, but she was making too much noise to be the enemy trying to sneak up on them. Enough noise that by the time she came into the camp itself, Aadet was there to meet her, face creased with worry. "Are you all right?" He glanced at the sky. Checking for the moon, she thought, as if he might have miscounted the days.

"Fine," Ree said, dropping onto the nearest pack. Something inside crunched at the impact. *I hope that wasn't important.* She wiped sweat and dirt from her forehead, grimaced, and wiped her hand off on her equally filthy pants. "Just half-killed myself getting here, and I expect I'll half-kill myself getting back, because there's a chance we can still catch them."

"You found the rebels? How?"

Ree shook her head. "Hell if I know. I mean, I *know*—I just can't explain it. There was a cat."

Aadet listened as she told the story. Listened, but didn't quite believe; she could see it in his expression. When she was done, he said, "You're telling me there's a magical leopard in this forest."

"She wasn't a leopard," Ree said, annoyed. "I've seen those. I know what they look like. Her head was too big and too square; her whole body was heavier, with shorter legs, and a much more powerful build. And did I mention the red eyes? I don't know what kind of cat it was—"

"A jaguar."

The answer didn't come from Aadet. Ree turned on her pack seat and saw Mevreš not far away. How long had he been standing there? His eyes were wide, his jaw hanging just a little bit slack, as if somebody had knocked him on the side of the head. "It was a jaguar."

"And you know this how?" Aadet said.

Mevreš swallowed, blinking as if he could restore his composure that way. "Because I think she saw a Korenat spirit. Vranatzin Iškovri."

"The Great Black One, with Eyes of Blood," Ree murmured.

She said it without thinking. *Jaguar*—that was one of the words she'd heard him say when he was counting the days. But she hadn't told Mevreš she was picking up the Korenat language; to him, her understanding would be just another piece of proof.

"Vrana—" Aadet said, then gave up. "This cat—this jaguar. What does it mean, and why would it show up to help Ree?"

She tensed, bracing for Mevreš to say it, the thing she'd held back from Aadet before the new moon. *She's Korenat.* Then Aadet would have questions, and all of that was a waste of precious time, when the rebels might vanish at any moment. But Mevreš only said, "There are two of them. Vranatzin Iškovri and Vlataltzin Iškonezal. They are . . . guardians of the path. With Vranatzin, it's the unknown path, the leap of faith into the darkness."

Like walking through the forest on a moonless night. "And the other?" Ree asked.

"The Great Bright One, with Eyes of Sun." Mevreš

held her gaze as he said it. Ree didn't bother pretending she hadn't known the translation; she was asking for the meaning of the spirit, not the words. "He is the path you can see, but will pay dearly to walk."

Maybe the other jaguar would show up when she and Mevreš sat down to talk again. "You say they're Korenat spirits. Did you pray to them for guidance while we're out here?"

"Yes. But they . . . even for an archon, they do not usually answer in so direct a fashion."

Aadet ran one hand through his hair. "All right. So in your opinion, we can trust this spirit's guidance."

"Absolutely," Mevreš said without hesitation. "Vranatzin does not play tricks. But she will demand blood."

It wasn't really funny, but Ree smiled anyway. "She ate three rebels. If that's not enough, I'm sure we'll have more for her pretty soon."

"Assuming we don't let these bastards slip away," Aadet said. He looked around the camp. They'd gathered quite an audience by then, the soldiers whispering among themselves about the spirit. That story would be hopelessly mangled by the time they heard it all, but Ree was too tired to care.

"We still have a little daylight left," Aadet said. "Pack fast. We're moving out."

• • •

Ree tried to catch Mevreš after that, but he seemed to be avoiding her. Angry about the language thing? Disappointed that Vranatzin had appeared to her but not to him? She couldn't tell, and she didn't have the energy to chase him down and force the point. Which might be a good thing, since it gave her time to think about whether she really wanted to.

They didn't get far before the fading light stopped them, but they were up again with the dawn, and more than halfway to the rebel encampment by noon. "When do you want to mount the attack?" Ree asked Aadet, during a brief pause on the march.

"Describe the area to me again." She did her best, allowing for the fact that she'd made her way there in pitch darkness. Aadet nodded. "I think I know the valley. If they're still there, we can move into position during the night and strike at dawn. That gives us a chance to do some reconnaissance and rest before the battle begins."

If anybody could scout the camp without being caught like she'd been, it was Aadet's people. Ree was stealthy enough, but nothing compared to these soldiers; they'd spent years in the mountains, while she'd only come and gone.

But the scouts came back too fast, crashing through

the underbrush like they didn't care who heard them. "They're on the move!"

This was the other gift of the soldiers' long experience: they responded without hesitation, seizing their weapons and gathering for Aadet's hurried commands. Ree gripped the hilt of her sabre and looked at Mevreš. "How good are you at fighting?"

"Not good enough. Go—don't worry about me."

She went.

Up the slope to a tall tree, where one of Aadet's people had already fixed a rope to a thick branch. A handful of daredevils were swinging across the knife-cut of the ravine to the other side, because they hadn't had the time to circle around and flank the rebels in any sane fashion. The soldier before her slipped on landing and skidded down into the ravine; Ree's *gemer* half, always present no matter the moon's phase, whispered that she stood a pretty good chance of breaking both of her legs. Her *seimer* half answered back, *Then I'll fight with the limbs I've got left.* Ree took the rope and launched herself across.

She didn't break her legs. She did wrench her knee, but after the first flare of pain she forgot the injury in the rush of battle. The other soldiers were already charging headlong for the exit from the ravine; Ree, following them, caught glimpses below of the fleeing rebels. It all depended on whether Sihpo Teglane was the sort to lead the escape, hoping to outrun Aadet's forces, or the sort to advance more cautiously and keep the flight from turning into a rout.

Ree didn't know. All she could do was stop as many of his men as possible. As the ravine rose to meet the surrounding terrain and the gap between the two groups shrank, a rebel came charging up the slope at Ree, machete in hand. She dropped into a slide and took out his hamstrings as she shot past, his blade whistling harmlessly over her head. Then she was down among the fleeing rebels and thought went away, lost in the chaos of battle.

It wasn't the kind of fight that had a clear end. She fought until nobody in sight was wearing armor marked with red rosettes; then she went toward the nearest sounds of steel and gunfire and fought some more. After a while Aadet's people began forming up into larger and larger groups, and then eventually there were no more red rosettes to find: they all lay dead or wounded, or had escaped into the forest.

Not all of the dead and wounded belonged to the Red Leopard. Aadet lost more than a tenth of his force in the hasty assault, and more than half of those who survived were bleeding or nursing twisted joints. Ree had a gash across her ribs she didn't remember taking. But Aadet himself had survived; her heart felt three times lighter when she glimpsed his familiar back through the trees. And Mevreš was alive, too, already tending to the wounded as they staggered or were carried in. *Would he have known if I died?*

The rebels were brought in, too, but not to be cared for. Aadet paced their ranks, examining faces and murmuring comments to one of his men, who made notes with a charcoal stick on a creased sheet of paper. Ree didn't recognize any of the captives, but Aadet picked out a few, officers from the previous army, high-ranking members of lineages that had supported the usurper. The rest were ordinary Solaine: leftovers from the old regime or youths who didn't remember a time before Valtaja.

"Did you get him?" Ree asked when he was done. "Is Sihpo Teglane among the prisoners?"

"No," Aadet said. "But there's at least a few I think were probably his lieutenants, so if nothing else, we cut off his arms."

"What about the turncoat? Was there one?" Mevreš had said there was, but until they had proof, it was nothing more than a theory.

Aadet sagged with weariness and disgust. "Sendje Teluo. He's dead—I think I'm glad."

Because that meant Aadet didn't have to confront him. Sendje Teluo; after a moment, Ree put the name to a face and a history. He'd been a low-level officer in Kaistun's guerilla force, always angling to be given a higher command, not a good enough tactician to merit the promotion. But he used to carve little animals at night out of scraps of wood, burning them in the cook-fire the next morning, and he'd guarded Aadet's back during the assault on Veiss.

Better for them all that he had died, rather than living to face the king's justice. Ree said, "So we just have to find out where Sihpo Teglane went."

"Maybe Mevreš can find out," Aadet said.

But the other archon shook his head when asked. "I can ask the Day Lords whether there will be more trouble in the future, if you like—once I'm done helping the wounded. But it won't point you in the direction he went."

In the end, they didn't need the Day Lords. Aadet's soldiers, retrieving the last of their dead from a fern-choked hollow, found the rebel commander among them, unconscious from a blow to the head. Aadet, obedient to his king's wishes, tried to carry the man out of the mountains, but he died without ever waking up. In the heat of a Solaine summer, nobody wanted to be lugging a corpse, and it wouldn't be fit for public display by the time it got to Taraspai. Instead they cut off his head and pickled it in a barrel brought for the purpose, and left the body for the carrion-eaters.

Ree hung back as the soldiers moved onward with their prisoners, waiting to see if Vranatzin came. But if the black jaguar claimed her last tribute, she did it after Ree was gone.

. . .

"You don't have to go," Aadet said. "Without you, we wouldn't have found the rebels, not that quickly. He'll forgive you overstaying his decree."

Ree wanted to believe him. It would have been nice to go back to Taraspai with Aadet and his soldiers and enjoy the fruits of their efforts: the praise, the gratitude, the free-flowing beer. But she couldn't risk it. "He's still establishing his power. Having an archon thumb her nose at his decree only a month after he made it . . . that wouldn't look good, no matter who I am. He'll be forced to show he meant what he said."

"He won't kill you. He *can't*. Not when you've helped him so many times."

She shrugged. "So he exiles me instead, and I can't come back to Solaike at all. It's better, but still not good. Look—" She laid a hand on Aadet's shoulder. "I'll wait in Cheot, just across the border. If Enkettsivaane invites me back for a parade, send a message and I'll come like a shot. If not, I'll move on. You'll see me again next year."

Aadet laid his hand over hers, gripping it tight. "Sooner than next year. I'll bring the message myself, one way or another."

There was never any question about whether Mevreš would leave. They all knew the king would be less inclined to grant leniency to him than to Ree. He'd said his goodbyes to the Nevati before he left to hunt the Red Leopard; he was already looking ahead, to the next group of Korenat. Still— "We owe you as well," Aadet said to him. "Who knows whether that cat would have led Ree to the camp without your prayers? I hope you'll come back someday."

Mevreš spread his hands. He was already masked, preparing for the journey north. "Perhaps. So long as the Nevati remain here, or any Korenat, there is a chance of it."

It's a good thing Aadet isn't the type to hear that as a threat, Ree thought. Because the reverse was also true: if they drove out the Nevati—or killed them—then that was one less archon they had to worry about in this land.

The two of them went north together, because Ree couldn't think of a good reason to separate, and wasn't entirely sure she wanted to anyway. Mevreš asked her for stories of her time with the revolutionaries; she told them, grateful for the safer topic. The unsaid words hung between them, and by the time they'd crossed the border, Ree was tired of carrying that weight.

On the outskirts of Cheot, Mevreš stopped and faced her. "Well. I will not wait around to hear whether the king will allow me back into Solaike; even if he does, it will likely be grudging at best. I suspect the courteous thing to do would be to vanish before his invitation arrives."

"Don't vanish just yet," Ree said, wondering whether he meant the word literally. *Stranger things are possible.* "I have something to tell you."

Mevreš waited. If he'd looked too expectant, too *smug,* she probably would have said "to hell with this" and walked away. But he only looked curious.

She ran her fingers down the loose edge of her sash. *Blood is the fundamental fact of the Korenat world.* This was what her blood had turned into, on the island of the Lhian: a strip of red fabric, an icon of her identity.

"The first time I saw you," Ree said, "on that quarry road, my body—it does this sometimes, not just around you. A feeling, like lightning in the blood. I felt it again when you counted the days, and when you talked to the king about what you are. About how the Korenat view the world."

If he'd guessed that already, he did a good job of hiding it. Very quietly, Mevreš said, "That is how the Day Lords speak to me—to any daykeeper. As I count the days, they answer with a feeling like that. I know their answer by where I feel it in my body: right side for male, left for female; the front of my body for the present, the back for the past, and so forth."

Ree had felt it all over, moving until it was almost everywhere at once. She looked away, into the green reaches of the mountains. "I believe what you said. Up here." She tapped her head. "But it doesn't *feel* right. It should resonate, shouldn't it? All I get is silence." Bitterness twisted the words. Mevreš embodied the blood ties that bound the Korenat together, and standing beside him, she felt more alone than she ever had.

"Come with me," he said. In her peripheral vision, she saw him twitch, as if he'd halted the impulse to touch her. "Spend time among your people. You know who they are, and have the freedom to join them; how many archai can say the same? You may begin to remember."

If he'd been confident, he would have said "you will remember." Ree turned back and met his gaze. "You feel it, too. There's something off."

He didn't deny it, which was admission all on its own. But Mevreš was undeterred. "Whatever your story is, the Korenat are the ones who told it. You belong with them."

Ree backed up a step; she couldn't help it. The word "belong" struck like a knife between the ribs. "You don't get it. So maybe I'm Korenat: that's nice. But I don't *be-*

long anywhere. I *can't*. What you're offering me—most people wouldn't say that's a home, not in the usual sense. It isn't a country or a town or even a house to call my own. But I can't sleep three nights in the same bed, and I can't have a home. Not with them, not anywhere."

Now she was the one planting a knife between his ribs. He wanted her to join them, with all the profound force of his nature. She couldn't accept for reasons just as profound. And however long he'd been in the world, however strong his gifts were, she would win that fight.

"Varekai," Mevreš said.

He'd never used that word in her hearing before. No one among the Nevati had, which meant she had no way of guessing its meaning. But it rang a bell deep within her mind, as if she'd heard it in another life. Apart from the blood, it was the one thing that felt anything like right. "What does that mean?"

"It's a term we use—a name of sorts. For those of the Korenat who go their own way, instead of walking with their kin." Mevreš nodded at her. "Like you."

Maybe she'd found the Korenat in ages past, and recognized herself as one of them. Or been recognized, by Mevreš or someone else, whether she felt the connection or not. But someone, somewhere, had called her Varekai before. In more than one lifetime, she thought.

"If you need me," Mevreš said, "then find any caravan

of our people and tell them to write my name on a slip of paper, wet it with their own blood, and burn it. I will know. And I will be there if I can." His gaze was steady and full of compassion. She wanted to shake it off like a fly, and cling to it at the same time.

He smiled, regretful and soft. "I hope you find your right path, Ree Varekai, wherever that may lead you."

Ree just nodded. She didn't trust her voice. Mevreš bowed to her in the Korenat style, then backed a few steps away. Then he was gone, vanishing just like he had said, his body curling away into smoke.

· · ·

She waited in Cheot until it was almost the new moon again. Aadet arrived on the last afternoon and found her sitting on the rim of the fountain at the center of town, picking leaves out of its waters.

"Let me guess," she said before he could even speak. "I'm not invited back."

"It was like you said," Aadet admitted. "He praised you for your obedience—you and Mevreš both. Exiling you would have been a display of power, but it would have made him look ungrateful. By leaving, you reinforced his authority."

"Well, I'm glad to be useful for something."

It wasn't the new moon yet, not until dawn the following day, but something of her *gemer* cynicism was already creeping in, brought on by her conversation with Mevreš. That side didn't rule her yet, though, and she had something to say before it did. "Besides, I have somewhere else to go."

"Off with Mevreš?"

She turned to look at him so fast, she almost fell off the fountain. "What?"

Aadet looked amused—and sad. "That thing you said, about him claiming he knew what you were. I figured it out, after that business with the cat. He thinks you're—"

"Don't say it." Ree cut him off, more weary than angry. "Yes. He does. And I think he's right, but . . . I don't *feel* it. He's gone his way, and I'm going mine."

"So if you aren't staying with him, then where *are* you going?"

She shook off one last, damp leaf, then wiped her fingers dry on her shirt. "Krvos."

The name meant nothing to Aadet, of course. "Where's that?"

"No idea," Ree said. "It's wherever the Korenat used to live, before they were driven out. Mevreš told me some stories—enough to figure it out, I think. I'm going to Krvos, or whatever the place is called now, and I'm going to see what happens when I get there." *If that doesn't make me remember, then nothing will.*

Aadet absorbed this in silence. Then he grinned. "All right."

His tone spoke of more than just understanding. Ree looked at him sharply. "You aren't going with me."

"Why not?"

"Because you're the king's wife. You have duties—"

"And he owes you. Since you weren't there to collect, I got his permission to come find you and give you whatever help you needed. Even if it meant leaving Solaike for a while."

It might be more than just a while. Ree opened her mouth to say she didn't need any help, but the words wouldn't come. She couldn't have a home, and she couldn't have a people . . . but she had a friend.

"Thanks," she said quietly. Then, driven by new energy, she sprang down from the fountain's edge. "It may be a long hunt. We'd better get started."

About the Author

MARIE BRENNAN is an anthropologist and folklorist who shamelessly pillages her academic fields for material. She is the author of several acclaimed fantasy novels including *A Natural History of Dragons;* The Onyx Court Series: *Midnight Never Come, In Ashes Lie, A Star Shall Fall,* and *With Fate Conspire; Warrior;* and *Witch.* Her short stories have appeared in more than a dozen print and online publications.

TOR·COM

Science fiction. Fantasy. The universe.

And related subjects.

*

More than just a publisher's website, *Tor.com*

is a venue for **original fiction, comics,** and

discussion of the entire field of SF and fantasy,

in all media and from all sources. Visit our site

today—and join the conversation yourself.